You're invited to a

CREEPOVER®

Your Worst Nightmare

D1516508

written by P. J. Night

SIMON SPOTLIGHT
New York London Toronto Sydney New Delhi

SIMON SPOTLIGHT
An imprint of Simon & Schuster Children's Publishing Division
1230 Avenue of the Americas, New York, New York 10020
Copyright © 2013 by Simon & Schuster, Inc.
All rights reserved, including the right of reproduction in whole or in part in any form.
SIMON SPOTLIGHT and colophon are registered trademarks of Simon & Schuster, Inc.
YOU'RE INVITED TO A CREEPOVER is a trademark of Simon & Schuster, Inc.
Text by Ellie O'Ryan
For information about special discounts for bulk purchases, please contact Simon & Schuster
Special Sales at 1-866-506-1949 or business@simonandschuster.com.
Manufactured in the United States of America 1113 OFF
First Edition 10 9 8 7 6 5 4 3 2 1
ISBN 978-1-4424-8235-7
ISBN 978-1-4424-8236-4 (eBook)
Library of Congress Control Number 2012956189

CHAPTER 1

"You don't have to wait, Mom," Kristi Chen said firmly. "I'll be fine. Just drop me off like it's a regular school day."

Mrs. Chen pursed her lips. "Are you sure, honey?" she asked. "It looks like the other parents are staying until the buses leave."

"But don't you have an important meeting?" Kristi replied. She actually couldn't remember if her mom had a meeting or not, but it was safe to assume that she did.

"Yes," Mrs. Chen admitted with a sigh. She glanced at her watch before she could stop herself. As one of the busiest lawyers in the state, Mrs. Chen was always rushing off to a big meeting or a court date.

"So go!" Kristi exclaimed. "Seriously, why waste your

time standing around breathing in bus fumes?"

"Okay," Mrs. Chen finally gave in. She wrapped her arms around Kristi for a big hug. "Be careful, Kristi. Don't go off by yourself; listen to your teachers; stay safe. I'll be out of town starting tomorrow for a deposition so I won't see you until Wednesday, but I told Tanya to pick you up at eight o'clock tomorrow night. Just call her if the buses are running late."

"Okay, Mom! Love you! Bye!" Kristi cried. She grabbed her overnight bag and backpack and bolted from the car before her mom could change her mind.

The rest of the seventh graders at Jefferson Middle School milled around the two buses that were idling by the curb. Kristi had never seen her classmates so excited to be at school on a Monday morning. She adjusted her backpack as she moved toward the crowd, looking for her best friend, Olivia Papas. But, as usual, Olivia found Kristi first.

"Kristi!" Olivia shrieked. "Are you psyched? I'm so psyched! I can't believe we're finally going on the field trip!"

"I know!" Kristi replied with a grin. Then she heard a familiar voice call out.

"Olivia! Kristi!"

Olivia's smile immediately disappeared. She grabbed

Kristi's arm and dragged her around to the other side of the bus. "Oh no. It's my parents . . ."

"Pretty bad this morning?" Kristi asked sympathetically.

"The worst ever." Olivia groaned. "They brought the video camera and they're *interviewing* kids about the trip. I'm gonna die of embarrassment."

Kristi couldn't help laughing. "I'm sorry," she said. "That's rough. But look on the bright side—at least they're not chaperoning."

"Shhh!" Olivia said, her eyes wide. "Don't jinx it. Besides, I won't believe that until the buses are moving and I *know* they're not on them! How'd you get rid of your mom?"

Kristi shrugged. "She had a meeting. The usual."

"Lucky," Olivia replied. "I wish my parents had a life . . . outside of ruining mine."

Just then the girls heard a loud whistle. "Attention, seventh graders," Mr. Tanaka, their social studies teacher, called above all the noise. "Please join me by the flagpole."

Everyone hurried over toward Mr. Tanaka. Ms. Pierce, the science teacher, stood next to him.

"At last, it's the day we've all been waiting for," Mr. Tanaka announced. "The annual seventh grade overnight field trip to Ravensburg Caverns is finally here!"

All the kids started cheering. Mr. Tanaka smiled indulgently for a moment before he raised his hands to quiet them.

"If you haven't already done so, please leave your luggage by the side of the bus so Mr. Carlson and Mr. Reed can load it. Remember, you can keep your backpack with you, but no eating or drinking on the buses," Mr. Tanaka continued.

"I'd like to remind everyone that even though we'll be away from school for two days, the regular school rules are still in effect," Ms. Pierce added. "If you break those rules, you *will* be sent home immediately."

Mr. Tanaka eyed the kids sternly for a moment, then he smiled. "Okay! If you're on bus one, please follow me. If you're on bus two, go with Ms. Pierce. And let's get this show on the road!"

"Hurry," Kristi said to Olivia. "I want to get a good seat. In the back."

The girls pushed their way through the crowd to bus one—but Mr. and Mrs. Papas stepped in front of them.

"One more hug!" Mrs. Papas cried as she reached for Olivia.

Olivia rolled her eyes as her parents squashed her in a giant bear hug, but only Kristi could see.

"We're going to miss you so much, Poodle," Mr. Papas said.

"Dad. You promised you would stop calling me that," Olivia said through gritted teeth. She glanced around to see if anyone besides Kristi had heard him. The nickname had been stuck to Olivia since second grade, when she used to wear her curly dark hair in two enormous, fluffy pigtails. Everyone at school already knew about it.

"Sorry," Mr. Papas apologized as he gave Olivia's hair a little tug. He turned to Kristi. "Take good care of each other, okay, Kristi?"

"Absolutely, Mr. Papas. You can count on me," Kristi said, trying not to laugh. "But we'd better go."

"I'm so bad at good-byes," Mrs. Papas said, wiping her eyes. "I love you, sweetie. Please be careful in the caves. I'm going to be so worried about you."

"Come on, Mom, I'll be back tomorrow night. You won't even notice I'm gone," Olivia replied. "Bye!" Then she hurried off to the bus, dragging Kristi behind her.

On the bus, Kristi spotted an empty row of seats that was almost at the back. Best of all, it was right in front of Julia Morales and Destiny Ryan, the most popular girls in seventh grade. Maybe she and Olivia could lean over the back of the seat and talk to them for the whole ride.

"Kristi, Kristi, wait," Olivia said, pulling Kristi over to a row on the opposite side of the bus—and right near the front. "Let's sit here."

"Here? In the front? Why?"

"Because my parents are taking pictures on the other side," Olivia explained. "They won't be able to see us if we sit over here. Please, Kristi? Please?"

Kristi sighed as she followed Olivia into the other row. Now they would be sitting just two rows behind Mr. Tanaka. It seemed pretty dumb to Kristi to pick a seat for the entire bus ride just because Olivia's parents wanted to take a couple of pictures of the bus leaving. But she knew how sensitive Olivia was about her parents, and how smothering they could be.

Olivia dug around in her backpack and pulled out her bright pink hairbrush. "Want me to do your hair?" she asked.

"Yes, please," Kristi replied. She twisted around in the seat so that her back was facing Olivia. Kristi closed her eyes as Olivia started brushing her long hair.

An obnoxiously loud voice rang through the bus. "Hey, look at that! Usually the poodle is the one being groomed!"

Kristi didn't need to open her eyes to know who was talking. She'd know that voice anywhere. "Hi, Bobby," she said.

"Actually, what she meant to say was, 'Shut up, Bobby,'" Olivia said.

But Bobby Lehman had never shut up in his life, and he wasn't about to start now. He threw his backpack into the seat in front of Kristi and Olivia. "Ooh, Olivia, will you do my hair next? Puh-leeease?" Bobby cooed in a high-pitched, squeaky voice.

Olivia shot Bobby a dirty look as she put down her hairbrush and started playing around with her phone. Almost immediately, Kristi's phone buzzed with a text from Olivia.

> K, u were so right about the seats. I wish
> we weren't stuck behind Bobby. UGH!

Kristi gave Olivia a little smile, but she didn't text her back. She knew Bobby could be really annoying. He was the youngest of four brothers and he always tried so hard to make everyone laugh. He was so desperate to be the center of attention all the time that it often backfired, and Kristi felt a little sorry for him. He didn't seem to have a lot of friends; even now, he was the only kid on the packed bus who was sitting all by himself. And Kristi never would have admitted it—not even to Olivia—but she actually thought Bobby was cute. Kinda. Sorta. And sometimes he was actually really funny. And when he wasn't trying to show off, Kristi thought he could be really nice, too.

"So are you guys looking forward to exploring the caves tomorrow?" Bobby continued as the bus pulled out of the school parking lot.

Olivia put on some headphones and started listening to music from her phone. There was no way that Bobby could've missed the hint, but he ignored it completely.

"I'm not," Bobby answered his own question. "Those caves are scary. Not fun scary, *really* scary."

"What do you mean?" Kristi asked curiously.

"My brothers told me all about it," Bobby said loudly.

"They said it should be *criminal* to take kids into the Ravensburg Caverns. After what happened there."

Kristi raised her eyebrows. She was pretty sure that Bobby was about to tell one of his over-the-top stories. But even so, she couldn't help asking, "What? What happened?"

"It was a long time ago," Bobby began as kids in other seats stopped chatting and started listening in. "Almost a hundred years ago, actually. Well, the caves were a really big deal even back then. Like, every day people lined up for a chance to go inside and see the wonders of the Ravensburg Caverns. And schools—just like our school—sent kids there on field trips."

"So?" yelled Evan Hollis from a few rows behind Kristi.

"So . . . ," Bobby said, pausing dramatically, "so . . . one time a class disappeared in the caves. Twenty-one kids. Vanished. Gone without a trace."

Now it seemed like just about everyone on the bus was focused on Bobby. Even Mr. Tanaka had shifted in his seat, like he was listening with one ear.

"The townspeople searched for *months*," Bobby said, leaning over the seat back. He had everyone's attention now and he was determined to keep it. "Even after they had lost all hope that the kids would be found alive, they kept looking. They brought in search-and-rescue dogs and they searched, and they searched . . . and they found nothing. Not a footprint. Not a fingerprint. Not a sweater. Not a hair bow. Not a body. Not even a bone. Twenty-one kids vanished off the face of the earth, as if they had never . . . even . . . existed."

"But what . . ." Kristi swallowed; her mouth was suddenly very dry. She tried again. "But what happened to them?"

Bobby shrugged. "Nobody knows. Most people think that they must have fallen into, like, an abyss or something. Some of those drops in the cave . . . Even now, they don't know quite how far they go down. But I don't think so."

"How come?" asked Olivia. Kristi wondered when Olivia had taken off her headphones.

"Come on," Bobby said confidently. "How would twenty-one kids all fall down the same hole? I mean, sure, two or three. Maybe even five. But wouldn't the ones at the back be able to save themselves? They weren't, like, babies. They were our age. So whatever happened to those kids was worse. Way worse. And my brother says . . ."

"What?" Kristi and Olivia exclaimed at the same time.

"My brother says that if you listen really carefully in the caves, you can still hear the echoes of their cries for help. *Please . . . please . . . please . . . help . . . help . . . help . . . meeeee . . . meeeee . . . meeeee . . .* ," Bobby said, raising his voice to a shrill whisper as he imitated the echoes.

The sound of Bobby's echoes made chills run down Kristi's neck. But apparently she was the only one who responded that way: Everyone else on the bus burst into laughter. It was definitely not the response Bobby was hoping for. His whole face darkened.

"Okay, okay, save it for Halloween, Mr. Lehman," Mr. Tanaka said sternly. "An excellent tall tale . . . but not a true one. You'll all learn about the real history of the Ravensburg Caverns on our tour tomorrow."

"It *is* true," Bobby said stubbornly. "I know a lot more about the caverns than you do."

"Watch it, young man," Mr. Tanaka said, and there was no mistaking the warning in his voice. "And face forward, please. No turning around in your seat while

11

the bus is moving—you know better."

Bobby slumped down in his seat. Kristi couldn't see him any longer, but she could imagine the frustrated look on his face. Just then her phone buzzed with another text:

Lame story, right?

Kristy half-smiled, half-shrugged at Olivia. "Hey, I downloaded some new songs last night," she said, changing the subject abruptly. "Want to listen?"

"Definitely!" Olivia exclaimed, plugging her headphones into Kristi's phone. Kristy cued up the first song and stared out the window while Olivia listened to it.

She couldn't stop thinking about the story that Bobby had told. The thought of being lost in the caves . . . lost forever . . . made her wish that she was in second-period Spanish class instead of heading straight for the Ravensburg Caverns. Because you could use a lot of words to describe Bobby—he was definitely a loudmouth, a bragger, an attention hog—but Kristi knew one thing: Bobby Lehman was no liar.

CHAPTER 2

A few hours later, the buses pulled up in front of the Ravensburg Motel. All the students screamed so loudly that Mr. Tanaka pretended to plug his ears. "We made it!" he joked. "Before we get off the bus, I want to remind everyone to be on their best behavior. We're not the only ones staying at the motel right now, so I expect each and every one of you to be respectful of the other guests. That means no yelling, no shrieking, no running—you know the drill. Now, when we get into the lobby, I want you to line up with your roomie so Ms. Pierce and I can distribute your room keys."

Kristi and Olivia exchanged a grin. "Come on, *roomie*," Kristi said with a giggle as she stood up and stretched. She was looking forward to moving around a little—six hours sitting on a school bus was about six hours too many!

Because of Mrs. Chen's busy schedule, Kristi and her family didn't get to go on vacation very often—but when they did, they stayed in nice hotels. Kristi had never realized just how nice those hotels were until she walked into the lobby of the Ravensburg Motel. Faded brown-and-orange curtains sagged across the windows, and the carpet was dotted with tiny holes and mysterious stains. Worst of all, the entire lobby smelled disgusting—worse than the cafeteria on sloppy-joe day. Olivia looked at Kristi and made a face.

"Maybe the rooms upstairs will be nicer," Kristi said hopefully.

"Maybe," Olivia repeated—but she didn't sound convinced.

"Chen, Kristi. Papas, Olivia," Ms. Pierce said, scanning over her roster as she walked up to them. She handed each girl a plastic key card. "You'll be in room two-twenty-two, on the second floor. The bus drivers are almost done unloading the luggage, so why don't you grab your bags and get settled into your room? Then everyone will have free time until five o'clock, when we'll meet at the motel diner for dinner. Remember, no one is allowed to leave the motel, got it?"

"Got it!" Kristi and Olivia replied. Then they found their bags and took them upstairs to room 222, where they soon realized that Kristi was wrong about their motel room. It was just as dingy as the lobby.

Kristi dumped her overnight bag on one of the beds and walked over to the window. She pulled back the peach-colored curtains and peered out the streaky window. Across the parking lot she could see the black, gaping mouth at the entrance to the Ravensburg Caverns. Even from a distance it looked cold and creepy . . . especially when Kristi remembered Bobby's story.

"I can't believe we're going *in* there tomorrow," she said.

"What, did Bobby scare you with his story?" Olivia teased her.

"I'm not scared," Kristi insisted. "But you have to admit that the cave sounds like a pretty freaky place. In a good way, I mean."

"Totally agree," Olivia said, nodding her head. "But come on. Let's go downstairs. This room looks even worse than the lobby and I think I saw a gift shop when we walked in."

Back in the lobby, Kristi spotted the diner around the back of the check-in desk. It had a blinking neon sign and a large chalkboard with the daily specials written on it.

TODAY'S SPECIALS: STROGANOFF, MIXED-MEAT STEW, MEAT-LOAF SANDWICH, MOLASSES COOKIES FOR DESSERT.

Kristi suddenly realized where the weird smell was coming from.

"*That's* where we're eating tonight? And tomorrow?" Olivia asked in disbelief.

"It must be," Kristi replied. "The sign in the window says FOOD."

"But it smells nothing like food," argued Olivia.

"Dog food, maybe!" Bobby said as he walked up to them. Despite themselves, Kristi and Olivia started to laugh.

"Come on," Olivia said to Kristi. "Let's go check out the gift shop."

Of course Bobby tagged along, as if Olivia had been talking to him, too.

"My mom gave me twenty dollars," Bobby announced.

"So I hope there's some cool stuff in the gift shop."

Before Kristi or Olivia could respond, Bobby suddenly burst forward and caught another boy, Tim Hendricks, in a headlock. "TIMMMMMMM-BERRRRRR!" Bobby yelled.

"Hey, hey, hey, get off!" Tim said, laughing as he tried to duck out of Bobby's grip. Tim was one of the most easy-going kids in the whole seventh grade (unless he was competing in a track event. Then he was a fierce competitor); not even Bobby's antics could faze him. "Chill, man."

"We're going to the gift shop. Wanna come?" Bobby asked.

Tim shrugged. "Sure, I guess. There's not much else to do around here, is there? The TV in my room only gets two channels."

They reached the gift shop and split up to explore. It was smaller than Kristi expected. Several of the shelves were empty. There was a small black cat curled up on one, sleeping in the late-afternoon light. "Hi, kitty," Kristi called to it. The cat chirruped and gave a big stretch, then went right back to sleep. Kristi continued to look around. Near the old-fashioned cash register she saw dusty glass jars filled with pale pink, green, and yellow rock candy. She could hear Bobby and Tim snickering nearby as they messed around with a shelf full of wind-up circus-animal toys. The toys still worked, even though they were pretty rusty. Again and again, the boys wound up the monkeys, elephants, and lions and faced them off so that they would crash into one another.

After walking around the store for a few minutes, Kristi joined Olivia in front of a locked display case. She gasped when she saw what was inside: an assortment of glittering stones, as big as plums and as red as blood.

"Are those *rubies?*" Kristi asked.

"I don't know," Olivia replied. "They're so pretty, aren't they? The best thing in this store. I was gonna buy one, but . . ."

As Olivia's voice trailed off she pointed at a small sign near the bottom of the case. In thick black letters, it read FOR DISPLAY ONLY!!! NOT FOR SALE!!!

"Wow," Tim said as he joined them. "Are those for real? I was looking at those geodes over there, but the ones they cracked open aren't as nice. They're just gray inside. They don't even have a lot of crystals."

Kristi moved away to look through a revolving rack of postcards. She hadn't seen anything that she wanted to buy yet, but maybe there would be some cool postcards she could bring home to show her mom. She slowly spun the rack around, but every card seemed kind of . . . creepy. There was one with a freaky-looking crow standing in the mouth of the caverns. It read: QUOTH THE RAVENSBURG CAVERNS . . . NEVERMORE. And there was another one with a photo that appeared to be taken at the edge of a bottomless pit. It said: I SURVIVED RAVENSBURG CAVERNS . . . COULD YOU?

Before Kristi could check out another postcard, someone shoved a brown paper bag in her face.

"What is—!" she exclaimed in surprise.

Bobby's face appeared above the bag. From the crinkles around his eyes, Kristi could tell that he was grinning. "Grab bag!" he announced. "Here. I got you one. I got one for everybody. They were only a quarter each."

Kristi glanced over her shoulder to see Tim and Olivia holding grab bags too.

"They're probably not going to be very good," Bobby babbled on. "Only a quarter. That's, like, nothing. But whatever. Might be fun. Or not. There's only one way to find out. Who wants to go first?"

"I will," Olivia said quickly, giggling a little as she stuck her hand into the wrinkled bag. She paused for a second before pulling out . . . a piece of cardboard with dented edges. Two long, sharp pins were stuck in it, securing a very large, very fuzzy, very dead moth.

"Ahhhhh!" Olivia shrieked. She frantically wiped her hand on her sweatshirt; her fingers were coated in translucent dust from the dead moth's wings. "Get it off! Get if off!"

"Ewwwww," Kristi said loudly, partly to cover Olivia's meltdown and partly because the dead moth *was* pretty gross. She reached for the moth and the bag so that Olivia wouldn't have to hold them for a moment longer.

"That was so—so—" Olivia stammered.

"Yuck," Kristi finished for her. She looked more closely at the moth. It was very pale, almost completely white, with unusual markings—jagged silver stripes intersected by splotchy gray circles. Kristi shoved the gross dead moth back into the bag. "Well, I guess I'll go next. I hope there's nothing *dead* in my bag!"

"Would you rather get a bug that was still alive?" Bobby joked.

Kristi plunged her hand into her grab bag. She felt several bumpy, oval-shaped objects, but didn't have a clue what they were. Her fingers closed around one and she pulled it out of the bag.

It was a miniature clown head. Its face was as white as death, with bloodred hair and lips and vacant blue eyes staring at . . . nothing. Instinctively, Kristi dropped the bag, only to watch in horror as a dozen more miniature clown heads bounced out of the bag and rolled around at her feet. The black cat that had been sleeping on a nearby shelf jumped down and began batting one of the clown heads around on the floor.

All the color drained from Kristi's face. She couldn't even speak. She started to back away from the clown heads, rolling and grinning at her with those bloody-looking mouths, when Olivia reached out and grabbed her arm.

That was all it took to remind Kristi that everything was okay. When their eyes met, Kristi could see sympathy and understanding in Olivia's gaze. She took a deep breath. Olivia was the only person at school who knew what had happened in the fun house, back in kindergarten, and Kristi was determined to keep it that way.

Tim knelt down and examined one of the clown heads. "Oh," he said, sounding a little disappointed. "They're just erasers . . . you know, pencil toppers."

"Oh. Duh," Kristi said as a flush of embarrassment crept up her cheeks. She tried to laugh. "Of course. I was just, like, *ahhhh*, there's a head in my hand!"

It worked. Everyone else started to laugh too. Tim and Bobby finished picking up the clown heads. Then Tim said, "Me next!"

His bag was bulging, filled nearly to the brim with whatever mystery item it contained. Tim stuck his hand in and pulled out a heaping handful of matchbooks. A few of them slipped through his fingers and tumbled to the floor.

"I don't—" Tim said, frowning at the matchbooks.

Kristi picked one up from the floor and looked at it too. The cover read GUARANTEED TO BURN HOTTER, STRONGER, AND LONGER! and there was an illustration of a grinning devil's head engulfed in a flame.

"Exactly what do you think you're doing?" said someone behind them.

It was Mr. Tanaka!

Kristi jumped a little as she shoved the matchbook

into her pocket. But Mr. Tanaka didn't even seem to notice that she'd been holding one. His eyes were focused on Tim, who had gone very pale.

"I'm extremely disappointed, Mr. Hendricks," Mr. Tanaka said sternly as he grabbed the matchbooks out of Tim's hand. He shook them in Tim's face. "You just broke a big school rule, young man. I *know* you know that matches are prohibited at all times. I have no choice but to send you home. Let's go call your parents. You can explain to them why they have to come pick you up."

"No—" Tim croaked.

"And then I think we'll call Principal Bryer," Mr. Tanaka continued.

"Mr. Tanaka, wait," Kristi said. She was so scared that Mr. Tanaka would find out that she had a matchbook too—she could practically feel it burning in her pocket—but she couldn't let Tim get in trouble for this. "It's not his fault. We got these grab bags—"

"I bought one. For everybody," Bobby interrupted her.

"And they were all filled with, like, really freaky weird things," Kristi spoke over Bobby. "Like mine had all these clown-head erasers. And Tim's was stuffed with matches. But he didn't know that until he looked inside."

"Is this true, Tim?" Mr. Tanaka asked.

Tim nodded vigorously. "Yeah. I had no idea my grab bag was full of matches. I would never bring matches on a school trip, Mr. Tanaka. Or buy them or anything like that. I know the rules. I promise," he said in a rush.

Mr. Tanaka was quiet for a long moment. Then he said, "Okay, Tim, I believe you. I'm sorry I jumped to conclusions. But I'll be taking these, if you don't mind"—the matches made a rustling noise as Mr. Tanaka took the bag from Tim—"and I think I'll have a word with the hotel manager about the contents of these, uh, 'grab bags.'"

"Thanks, Mr. Tanaka," Tim said gratefully. "I never wanted them to begin with." As soon as Mr. Tanaka had turned away, Tim sighed with relief.

"Man, I'm sorry about that," Bobby said right away. "So sorry, dude."

"Whatever," Tim said. He shrugged, like it really didn't matter, but Kristi could see that he still looked pale. "Not your fault. No big deal."

"No, it is," Bobby argued. "You could've gotten in serious trouble."

"But I didn't," Tim replied, a hint of annoyance creeping into his voice. "Can we drop it?"

"Bobby, what's in your grab bag?" Kristi asked quickly.

"Oh. Right. I almost forgot to look," Bobby said. He shook the bag gently. "Whatever it is, it's pretty light."

The three other kids watched as Bobby peered into the bag. It was hard to read the expression on his face. Finally, he looked up. "Nothing," he reported, holding the bag upside down and shaking it to prove that it was empty. "What a rip-off."

"At least they were only a quarter," Olivia pointed out. "Come on, it's almost time to meet for dinner . . . or whatever they're serving in that diner."

As the friends wandered out of the gift shop, Kristi drifted toward the back of the group. She paused as they passed by the cashier; then, in one fast motion, Kristi dropped the clown heads, the moth, and the book of matches onto the counter. The cashier gave her a curious look.

But Kristi didn't even notice. She didn't want anything to do with the "gifts" in those grab bags.

CHAPTER 3

At dinner Kristi ordered the meat-loaf sandwich, hoping that it would be halfway decent. One bite told her that she was wrong. She scraped the soggy gray meat off the sandwich and ate the bread instead, thankful for the generous portion of French fries and coleslaw on the side of her plate. When Kristi glanced around the diner, she saw that most of the other kids had done the same.

"This molasses cookie is actually awesome," Olivia said during dessert. "I'll be honest, I'm surprised."

"Well, it would be hard to make anything taste worse than that meat loaf," Kristi joked.

Afterward, Mr. Tanaka, Ms. Pierce, and the chaperones herded everyone into a conference room on the second floor for the most ridiculous game of charades that Kristi had ever played. A few of the kids from the drama club got really into it, but everyone else seemed bored—or at least pretended to be.

"How long are they going to keep us here?" Olivia whispered.

"Ugh, I don't know. Until lights out?" Kristi guessed. She glanced at her watch. It was only eight thirty. That meant they could be stuck playing charades for another hour!

"We're not babies," Olivia replied. "They don't need to entertain us every second."

"It could be worse," joked Kristi. "At least we're not playing heads up, seven up!"

Finally, at nine o'clock, Mr. Tanaka told everyone that they could go to their rooms and get ready for bed. "But remember, lights out is in half an hour," he reminded them. "And we *will* be checking."

Kristi and Olivia walked down the hall to their room.

"That was so lame. And I'm not even tired," Olivia said. "I can't believe we're supposed to go to bed at nine thirty. Isn't this, like, supposed to be a vacation?"

"Well, Mr. Tanaka said 'lights out,'" Kristi said slowly as she opened the door to their room. "He didn't say 'go to sleep.'"

Olivia grinned at her. "Good point! We can still text people and stuff, huh?"

"Yeah, I don't see—" Kristi began.

Suddenly the hotel phone on the nightstand rang. Both girls jumped.

"Who do you think it is?" Olivia asked. "Should we answer it?"

"I guess so," Kristi replied. "What if it's somebody from home?"

She lifted the receiver and said, "Hello?"

There was a long silence. Then an unfamiliar male voice said, "Kristi Chen?"

"Yes, this is Kristi," she replied.

"This is the hotel manager. You know why I'm calling, don't you?"

"Um, no," Kristi replied as her heart started to beat a little faster. She racked her brain, trying to think of anything she'd done that might get her in trouble. "I honestly have no idea."

"I think you know."

The matches, Kristi suddenly thought. *Somebody saw me put the matches in my pocket and they think I stole them. And they're gonna tell Ms. Pierce and Mr. Tanaka, and Mom will have to pick me up from here and she'll be so mad at me—and everyone will think I'm a thief—*

Kristi cleared her throat. "Please," she replied. "Please tell me."

There was a long silence. Then the person on the other end dissolved into giggles—and hung up the phone!

Kristi stared at the phone in her hand for a moment before she started laughing too. Then she hung up.

"*What* was that about?" Olivia asked.

"Prank call!" Kristi exclaimed. "I can't believe they got me. I wish I knew who it was! I totally didn't recognize the voice at all."

"Maybe it was Tim." Olivia guessed.

"Maybe," Kristi said. "I wonder if he has that voice-disguise app on his phone?"

"Oh, he totally does," Olivia said, nodding vigorously. "I know it for a fact."

"How rude!" Kristi said—but she wasn't really mad.

The phone rang again.

"Let me get it!" Olivia cried as she lunged for the phone. "Hello? Hello?"

With a slight frown, she hung up. "Nobody's there."

Then there was a loud knock at the door. Both girls had silly grins on their faces.

"Okay, this is getting ridiculous," Olivia said. "I'm going to tell them to leave us alone—"

"Wait, don't answer it!" Kristi exclaimed. "Not until you look through the peephole."

"Oh, right," Olivia said. She peered through the little hole in the door, then turned around and walked back to the bed. "Nobody's there. Again."

There was another knock, and goose bumps spread down Kristi's arms.

"This is getting kind of weird," she said. "Should we—should we call Mr. Tanaka? Or Ms. Pierce?"

"Don't get freaked out over nothing," Olivia replied. "Just ignore it."

But when the knock came a third time, Kristi couldn't resist. She strode over to the door and flung it open.

Sure enough, there was no one there. But there was *something* there.

A brown paper bag, sitting in the doorway.

Not another grab bag, Kristi thought with dread. She still hadn't totally recovered from those creepy clown heads.

Her name was printed on the bag, in thick block letters.

"What is it?" Olivia asked as she came up behind Kristi.

"Another grab bag," Kristi replied. "I don't even want to open it."

"But you have to," Olivia said. "It has your name on it."

"Let's open it together," Kristi suggested.

Olivia shrugged. "Sure. Whatever."

Kristi carefully opened the bag. At the same time, both girls peered inside it. Then they started laughing. The bag was filled with rock candy!

"Well, that's a relief," Kristi said.

"Totally, except we can't eat it. It's all dusty. It's probably been in that gift shop since our grandparents were kids!" Olivia giggled. "Hey, look—there's something else written on the back."

It was a short note, in the same block handwriting.
SORRY THE GRAB BAGS WERE LAME.

"Whoa. You know what this means, right?" Olivia asked. "This is from *Bobby*! Bobby got this for you! I bet Bobby *likes* you!"

"Shut up. He does not," Kristi said as she felt the back of her neck get hot.

"He so does!" crowed Olivia. "It's obvious! I mean, *my* grab bag was really lame too, and he didn't bring *me* any candy!"

"Yeah, because he figured we would share!"

"But *my* name isn't on the bag," Olivia pointed out.

"Liv. Please, please, please don't tell anybody, okay?" Kristi begged. "Let's just—let's just forget it."

Olivia immediately grew serious. "Of *course* I wouldn't tell anybody!" she exclaimed. "I would never do that to you. God, how embarrassing. Bobby Lehman, like, *loves* you. Don't worry, nobody will find out from me."

"Good. I'm gonna go brush my teeth," Kristi said.

In the bathroom, Kristi stared at herself in the mirror as she brushed her teeth. Her mind was racing. *Is it possible?* she wondered. *Can Bobby really have a crush on me? I hope Olivia won't say anything to anybody . . . and I really hope she didn't guess that I kind of like him, too.*

After Kristi finished in the bathroom, there was

another knock at the door—but this one was quickly followed by Ms. Pierce's voice. "Lights out in five minutes, girls!" she called through the door.

"Okay!" Kristi and Olivia replied.

"So . . . do you want to text Tim?" Olivia whispered after the girls had climbed into their beds. "And tell him that his prank call was totally stupid?"

"Ehhh . . . you can," Kristi replied. "I'm really tired. I might just go to sleep."

"Oh," was all that Olivia said, but Kristi couldn't miss the disappointment in her voice. "Okay. Night, Kristi. See you in the morning."

"Night, Liv," Kristi replied as she turned out the light.

The soft glow from Olivia's phone illuminated the room. Kristi was glad. Sometimes, when she was home alone at night because her mom was working late, Kristi went to sleep with the hall light on. And tonight, lying on a lumpy, musty mattress in the Ravensburg Motel, Kristi felt that same gnawing loneliness in the pit of her stomach, even though Olivia was just a few feet away.

She suddenly missed the familiar sounds of her

own house, the familiar smell of her own sheets, the familiar feel of her own bed.

Kristi squeezed her eyes shut tight . . . and fell asleep faster than she expected. Instantly, she began to dream. . . .

She was in an unfamiliar place—a place that was equal parts shadow and rock, neither indoors nor outdoors. Not sure what to do, she started to walk. One step, then another, the empty echo of her footsteps was the only sound she could hear.

Where am I? *she wondered.*

Kristi had no idea.

The intensity of her longing to escape, to go home, was unexpected. It wasn't such a bad place—wherever she was. It was quiet. It was cool, but not cold. She was alone, but that wasn't so bad.

Was it?

Then, suddenly, Kristi stopped. She thought she heard something—there it was again—

Footsteps.

Someone was walking behind her.

Someone who stopped when she stopped, moved when she moved. That someone didn't want her to know that she was being followed, but she knew. She knew. And that was enough to make Kristi start running. She didn't turn around to see who was chasing her. Somehow she had figured out who it was, and if Kristi caught a glimpse of that white face, that wig, that jagged grin, that horrible makeup, she would be too terrified to move. But some locked-away corner of her mind was jangling with unease, because this did not match her memory, not at all: She was definitely not in the fun house.

Then why was the clown chasing her?

Because that's the thing about your worst nightmare; Kristi had figured it out a long time ago. Whatever scares you the most is always waiting to rise up and find you. It will be there, waiting for you, when you least expect it.

It was hard to run in the dark, but Kristi tried—oh, how she tried—but her legs were like lead and her blood was like ice. Her own body had turned against her, but her brain refused to accept it, refused to admit defeat. Silent screams shook her skull and yet every nerve, every muscle, every fiber of her body ignored them. Move, she told herself. Move. Move. Move. She stumbled forward, a shambles of uncoordinated jerks and twitches. It would be so easy to stop running, but Kristi was determined to keep going.

There was one thing she hadn't expected though: the hands that suddenly shoved her, hard. Now she was falling, and running was no longer an option.

Solid ground slipped away, and she plunged through the

endless dark: flailing arms, thrashing legs. Kristi was desperate to grab on to anything, but there was nothing to hold. Her ears filled with the rushing wind as she fell, and something else, something worse, the echo of long-ago cries for help, for mercy. They were growing louder, closer—surely, surely the end was near, and until then Kristi could do nothing but scream . . . and wait for it all to be over.

CHAPTER 4

"Kristi!" Olivia whispered frantically. "Wake up! Wake up!"

Gasping, Kristi tried to sit up but something—someone—was holding her down. "Let me . . . go . . . get off . . . ," she mumbled.

"You're dreaming. It's just a dream," Olivia said, her voice trembling with fear. "Open your eyes and look at me, Kris. I'm right here."

At first everything was blurry; the light overhead was blinding. *Light,* Kristi realized. *I'm not in the dark place anymore.* She tried to take a deep breath and sit up. A tangle of sweaty sheets wrapped around her waist and legs pinned her to the floor.

Kristi blinked and wiped at her bleary eyes. They

were watering, or else she had been crying. "Why am I on the floor? What happened?" she asked, and her voice was as hoarse as if she'd really been screaming.

Maybe she had.

"You fell out of bed," Olivia said. She started biting her cuticles. "You had a nightmare, huh?"

Kristi nodded slowly. "Yeah. I was—I think I was in a cave. But that wasn't the scary part, Liv. The fear I felt—it was just like I was back in the fun house."

Olivia made a sympathetic face. "The fun house again?"

"I don't know why I can't forget it," Kristi whispered. "But there I was, in the dark, trying to find a way out. I was so scared I could barely move, and there was some-one following me. I tried to run, but he . . . he . . . he pushed me off a cliff. I started falling and it was endless, like I was plunging through this bottomless pit."

"That sounds so scary," Olivia said. "All I know is I was sleeping and suddenly I woke up— I heard this hor-rible noise—"

"Yes!" Kristi cried. "Me too! The cries for help—oh my God, Liv, who is that? Is somebody in trouble—in the motel—"

Olivia looked at her blankly. "Kristi," she said. "It was you. You were—I don't know, not yelling, but kind of shrieking in your sleep. . . ." Olivia leaned back and wrapped her arms around her knees, hugging herself. "It was really freaky."

"No, that wasn't me," Kristi argued. "I *know* that wasn't me. I can still—I can still *hear* the screams. Listen . . ."

The two girls sat in an uncomfortable silence, straining their ears.

"I don't—" Olivia began.

"Shhh!" Kristi hissed. "You don't hear that? That haunted—that *howling* sound—it's faint, but I know it's there."

Olivia shook her head. "I don't hear anything now that you're awake."

Suddenly a look of horror flooded Kristi's face. She crossed the room and used all her strength to push open one of the windows. A rush of night air, damp and cold, poured over her. "Come here," she said. "Listen. It's definitely coming from outside."

Olivia stood next to Kristi by the window, shivering in her lime-green pajamas.

"You *have* to hear it," Kristi said, a note of desperation creeping into her voice. "*Listen*, Olivia! Just *listen!*"

"Okay, fine, I hear it," Olivia finally replied. "I mean, I think I hear it. But you were also screaming in your sleep."

Kristi ignored that last part. "I *knew* I wasn't imagining it!" she cried. "Should we—should we get some help? Tell Mr. Tanaka or—or—" Kristi had to swallow hard before she could continue. "It's *them*, isn't it?"

"'Them'? I don't know what you're talking about," Olivia replied. "That noise isn't coming from people. It's probably just, like, something from the caves."

Kristi gave her a look. "That's what I'm trying to say! Those kids—the ones Bobby told us about on the bus! The ones who went missing a long time ago. He said—remember? He said that you can still hear their cries for help!"

"No way," Olivia said bluntly. Then she started to laugh. "Look at you! You're freaking out over *nothing*! I can't believe you took Bobby's stupid story so seriously! He was just messing with everybody!"

When Kristi didn't respond, Olivia kept talking. "What I meant was, something *natural* coming from the caves," she continued. "Like wind blowing over the entrance. Or across one of the chasms. That's why it sounds so echoey. Like screaming."

"You really think so?" Kristi asked doubtfully. It sure didn't sound like a noise that could come from rocks and wind—but then again, she wanted so badly to believe that Olivia was right. . . .

"Definitely," Olivia said, sounding more and more confident. "Look at it this way—if it really was the sound of children screaming, we wouldn't be the only ones to hear it. I mean, people live in Ravensburg. They'd call the police and we'd be seeing cop cars and flashing lights and stuff. I'm sure it's nothing. Really."

"Okay." Kristi gave in. Olivia's theory was a lot better than the alternative.

Olivia yawned loudly. "We should try to go back to sleep," she said. "Mr. Tanaka said we're meeting for breakfast at six thirty. That's in three hours."

"Yeah, of course," Kristi said. "Sorry I woke you up, Liv. That must have been pretty frightening."

"Don't even worry about it," Olivia replied. "I just hope you don't have any more nightmares tonight."

"You and me both!" Kristi said, which made both girls laugh.

Olivia turned off the light. "Night, Kris."

"Night, Liv."

Kristi pulled the musty comforter under her chin and squeezed her eyes shut. She felt so tired, so deeply bone-tired, but was too scared to sleep. What if her dream picked up right where it left off? The darkness . . . the falling . . . those cries . . .

Just before dawn, Kristi finally fell asleep. But it seemed like only moments passed before Olivia was shaking her awake again.

"Breakfast is in five minutes, Kris," Olivia said in a sleepy voice. "I hope they have pancakes. Come on, you've gotta get up now."

"Okay, okay, okay," Kristi mumbled. "I'm up."

As fast as she could, Kristi took a two-minute shower, then put on her jeans and a black T-shirt. Before she ran out of the door, she grabbed her favorite red sweater, the one with the shiny buttons that seemed to glow when they caught the light.

"Better bring your sweatshirt," Kristi said to Olivia. "It might be cold in the caverns."

"Good idea," Olivia replied as she reached for the sweatshirt she had worn the day before. Then the girls walked downstairs to the diner. To Olivia's delight, they *were* serving pancakes, and breakfast tasted a lot better than dinner had the night before. Kristi wasn't very hungry, but she tried to eat as much as she could. The diner was bright and cheerful; the room was filled with the smell of warm maple syrup and sizzling bacon and all around her the other seventh graders were chatting and laughing excitedly. Everyone seemed to be having a great time. . . . Everyone except Kristi.

It was just a dream, she reminded herself for the thousandth time. *Shake it off. It was just a stupid dream.*

"Hey, guys," Bobby said as he slid into the girls' booth with Tim right behind him. Bobby gave Kristi a shy smile. "Did you guys have a good night? *Sweet* dreams, I mean?"

Panic flashed through Kristi's eyes. *How does Bobby know about my nightmare?* she thought wildly.

"Oh, the candy?" Olivia asked. "Yeah, it was, um, delicious."

Bobby's whole face lit up. "Awesome," he said, grinning. "I felt bad about those grab bags. Man, those things were so lame. So I was hoping you would like the candy."

"Thanks, Bobby," Kristi said. "That was really nice of you."

Just then Ms. Pierce stood up in the middle of the restaurant. "Let's finish up, people," she called out. "Our tour starts in fifteen minutes."

The excited chatter grew even louder as all the kids jumped up and pushed their way toward the exit, where the chaperones were waiting. As Kristi and Olivia moved toward the doors, Bobby tagged along behind them.

"You guys. Hang on," Tim said. He pointed at the table, which was cluttered with used napkins and dirty plates. "You didn't tip your waitress."

Olivia and Kristi exchanged a glance. "I thought all our meals were paid for," Olivia replied. "That's what the flyers about the field trip said."

"Yeah, but you've always gotta tip your waitress," Tim said firmly.

Kristi dug around in her pocket and put a handful of change on the table. So did Bobby and Olivia. Tim shook his head at them.

"Weak, guys," Tim said. He scooped up the change, pocketed it, and placed a five-dollar bill under the sugar dispenser.

"Timbo! Let's go! Timbo! Let's go!" Bobby bellowed right next to Kristi's ear. She flinched and tried to move her head away, but Bobby kept screaming Tim's name until Mr. Tanaka got involved.

"Settle down, Bobby," Mr. Tanaka warned him.

"Yes, sir. Aye, aye, captain," Bobby replied as he gave Mr. Tanaka a dorky salute. Olivia started laughing at him. Kristi cringed a little. She could not figure out what made Bobby act so, well, *clueless* all the time. Outside, the sun hadn't fully risen yet. A chilly mist seeped from the woods, wrapping itself around cars, trees, and shrubs. It was springtime, but it still felt like winter. Kristi shivered; she was glad she had remembered to wear her sweater.

"I hope it's not this cold in the caves," Olivia said as she stuck her hands in the pouch pocket of her sweatshirt.

"Me too," Kristi replied.

A stumpy-looking middle-aged woman was waiting for them at the entrance to the Ravensburg Caverns. "Jefferson Middle School?" she asked as she glanced down at the clipboard in her hand. Ms. Pierce nodded and shook the woman's hand. "Welcome to the

Ravensburg Caverns. I'm Mrs. Hallett, and I'll be your guide through the caves today. Please follow me."

As the students stepped through the gaping mouth of the entrance, a hush settled over them. Kristi craned her neck to look around. The rock walls soared overhead, rough with mineral deposits and streaks of sparkling mica. A few lightbulbs enclosed in wire cages dangled from a cord strung along the wall. They cast long, flickering shadows throughout the dim cave, hardly cutting through the dark gloom. It was even cooler— and creepier—than Kristi had imagined it would be.

"Squeeze in, everybody. Right next to your neighbor," Mrs. Hallett announced. "It's a tight fit in the entryway, but this is where we like to tell you a little bit about the Ravensburg Caverns before your tour."

Mrs. Hallett hadn't even finished speaking before Bobby's hand shot into the air. "I have a question," he said loudly. "Is it true that early settlers used the caves as prison cells? Because I read that there are these, like, rooms with old bars on them, and the settlers would lock up murderers and horse thieves and leave them there to die!"

A tight smile crossed Mrs. Hallett's face. "You're

mixing things up. The Ravensburg Caverns were discovered in 1739, when the first settlers in the area were prospecting for gold. Of course, they never found any—but I think we can all agree that the Ravensburg Caverns are *far* more valuable than a few gold nuggets, can't we?"

"Uh, hardly," Tim muttered under his breath, making Bobby snort with laughter.

Mrs. Hallett glared at him. "According to the diary of Captain Miles Larsen, a suspected thief took refuge in the caverns rather than face justice for his crimes, but he certainly wasn't *imprisoned* here. Most likely, he escaped through an alternate tunnel out of the caverns . . . or else he met with an accidental death. The Ravensburg Caverns have always been a treacherous place—but if you respect them, they will respect you."

Olivia gave Kristi a subtle nudge. "She's kind of nuts, huh?" Olivia whispered.

"Seriously. Maybe she spends too much time underground," Kristi whispered back.

"Now, you'll learn all about the *real* history of this astonishing natural wonder," Mrs. Hallett promised, "but I like to start at the beginning. We're standing at the uppermost part of the Ravensburg Caverns, a series of tunnels and rock chambers that continue for thousands of feet underground. Scientists think that the caverns were first formed when—"

Once again Bobby raised his hand. "Are you going to tell us about Circus Atrocitas?" he said. "Because what I heard was that they used to practice their top secret routines here so that nobody would know . . . but something went really wrong during one of their shows and, like, seventeen people in the audience *died*! And everyone in town was so mad they chased all the performers into the caverns . . . and they were never seen again!"

Mrs. Hallett wasn't smiling anymore. "The Circus Atrocitas accident was a long time ago and it had nothing to do with the Ravensburg Caverns," she said. "Now, if I could please continue, scientists think that the caverns were formed over many thousands of years. And do you know what created them?"

"Monsters?" Evan cracked, making everyone giggle.

"*Rain!*" Mrs. Hallett said loudly.

Ms. Pierce nodded. "Do you remember learning about this in class?" she asked the seventh graders. "Since rain is slightly acidic, it can dissolve minerals in limestone, forming an extensive network of caverns over time."

Mrs. Hallett cleared her throat; she looked annoyed by the interruption, even if it was from a teacher. "Today, you'll find that the caverns are home to a unique ecosystem of cave-dwelling creatures—" she tried to continue.

"From the toxic waste buried right under us!" Bobby practically yelled. "And now everything that lives here is a radioactive mutant! Have you seen them, huh? The mutants? Do they really glow in the dark?"

A bunch of kids started to laugh.

"Bobby," Mr. Tanaka said with a warning in his voice.

"There are no mutants here," Mrs. Hallett snapped. "I think you've been reading too many comic books, young man."

A dark cloud crossed Bobby's face. "Well, all those kids who disappeared weren't in any comic books," he muttered—just loudly enough to be overheard.

"That's it, Bobby," Mr. Tanaka said. "Enough. One more interruption out of you, and I'll be on the phone with your mother, and you'll miss out on the tour. Do you understand me?"

Bobby clamped his mouth shut as he nodded his head. Out of the corner of her eye, Kristi could see his ears turning bright red. *He always does this,* she thought, shifting on her feet so that she was standing a little farther away from him. *He totally brings it on himself. I don't know why, but he does.*

"Is it just me, or is Bobby even *more* annoying than usual?" Olivia whispered to Kristi. "What is going on with him?"

Kristi shrugged. "I don't know," she whispered back. "Maybe he's just excited about going into the caves."

Mrs. Hallett smiled again—smug and satisfied. "If there won't be any further *interruptions,*" she said, staring directly at Bobby, "let's go over the safety rules. As you can see, we've installed modern electrical lighting along the tour path. Not only will this help you see all the wonders of the caverns, it will help you stay safe: Any area *without* lights is strictly off-limits. No running or reckless behavior. You must stay *behind* the guardrails at all times. Some of the chasms we'll encounter are hundreds of feet deep, and a fall into one would be fatal. We might see some of the caverns' full-time occupants— the animals I mentioned before. If we do, you must not startle them. Please try not to make too much noise; we haven't had a rockslide in here for nearly thirty years and I'd rather not have one today."

Mrs. Hallett paused as she glanced around the group to make sure everyone was listening. The students were hanging on to her every word, completely mesmerized by her warnings about the dangers of the cavern.

"Finally, touch nothing and take nothing. There is a *lovely* gift shop in the Ravensburg Motel where you can buy *beautiful* geodes and *real* fossils if you'd like a souvenir from your visit today." Mrs. Hallett paused. "And now, if everyone is ready, let's begin the tour."

CHAPTER 5

Mrs. Hallett led the seventh graders down a sloping ramp that was bordered on both sides by metal guard-rails. Kristi peeked over one: the drop was about ten feet, a steep fall but not enough to kill anybody . . . she hoped. As if they were influenced by the subterranean stillness of the cave, the kids started speaking in hushed whispers that were hardly louder than their footsteps.

"Ravensburg Caverns is a series of underground chambers constructed out of ancient rock formations," Mrs. Hallett said as she walked. "Some of these chambers are enormous, with fifty-foot-high ceilings. Others are smaller than a broom closet. There are dozens of twisting tunnels that link these chambers; a few serve as exits out of the caverns."

"Mrs. Hallett," Mr. Tanaka said. "Sorry to interrupt, but can you tell us how many chambers there are?"

"I'm afraid not," Mrs. Hallett said, "because we simply don't know. There are at least sixty that have been explored, but some of the caverns we've found are made of unstable rock formations. They are simply too dangerous to enter, and there's no way to know what lies on the other side of them."

Suddenly Mrs. Hallett held up both hands to stop the group from walking further. "I have to ask you to be very, very quiet as we enter the next chamber," she said in a soft voice. "The Ravensburg Caverns are home to many creatures, including troglophiles, trogloxenes, and troglobites. Who can guess what those are?"

For a moment Bobby looked like he wanted to say something—but one look at Mrs. Hallett's face convinced him to keep his mouth shut.

"No, they aren't dinosaurs," Mrs. Hallett said, wagging her finger at Bobby—even though he hadn't said a word. She was the only one who laughed at her joke. "A *troglophile* is an animal that usually lives in a cave, but can leave the cave from time to time if it wants.

Troglophiles can include beetles, millipedes, centi-pedes, and other creepy-crawly creatures. They prefer dimly lit areas and will rarely venture into bright light. Then, of course, there are trogloxenes—animals who live in the cave, but have to leave it to find food. And a *troglobite*—"

A thin smile snaked across Mrs. Hallett's face. "Well, we'll talk about those a little later. The next room of the caverns is home to hundreds of trogloxenes. Or, as they're more commonly known in this case—*bats*."

Some of the girls squealed, but Mrs. Hallett silenced them with a stern look and a finger to her lips. "They're sleeping right now . . . or, at least, they *should* be. So if you're quiet as we pass through their chamber, they shouldn't bother us. I hope!"

Kristi turned to Olivia and rolled her eyes—but to her surprise, Olivia seemed pale. "You okay?" Kristi whispered.

"Ask her something for me?" Olivia said in a rush.

But it was too late. Mrs. Hallett was already walk-ing into the next chamber and the seventh graders were following. The lights seemed even dimmer here, or per-haps the impossibly high cave ceilings somehow sucked up most of their brightness. There was still enough light, however, for Kristi to see them: bats, hundreds of them, *thousands* of them, hanging above their heads, from every ledge and rocky outcropping in the chamber. Wrapped in their wings, the bats' bodies swayed as they slept, rocked by an invisible current of air.

Why? wondered Kristi. *How? How is there a breeze in here, underground? Where could it be coming from?*

Every so often one of the bats stretched in its sleep, unfurling those leathery wings before wrapping itself up again and falling back into a fitful doze. Kristi had the sense that they slept lightly, very lightly, and that it wouldn't take much commotion to wake them. To imagine it was awful—the rushing wings beating over their heads as panicked, angry bats fled the cave, flying low with fangs bared and talons tangled in the kids' hair and hoodies.

Luckily, her classmates seemed to sense that too, and everyone was silent as they moved—faster than usual—through the bats' chamber.

On the other side, Kristi breathed a sigh of relief. Then she turned to Olivia. "What did you want me to do?"

"Can you ask her about moths?" said Olivia.

"Huh? Ask her *what* about moths?" Kristi replied.

"You know. If there are *moths* in the cave," Olivia said impatiently. "Those troglo-whatevers she wouldn't tell us about. Maybe they're a kind of horrible moth like that thing that was in my grab bag."

"Ohhhh," Kristi said, nodding. No wonder Olivia looked so pale. Kristi had never really understood her best friend's phobia of moths, but she knew what it was like to be so terrified of something that it was hard to even talk about it. So she didn't hesitate to raise her hand.

"Yes, girl in the red sweater?" Mrs. Hallett said.

"I was wondering if any moths live in the Ravensburg Caverns," Kristi said.

"Moths?" Mrs. Hallett said. "Oh, probably. Near the entrance of the caves, like the bats. Moths are less adapted for deep cave life than other creatures."

Kristi glanced at Olivia to give her a reassuring smile, but her friend still looked worried. So Kristi pressed on.

"But what about the, um, troglobites," Kristi continued. "Are some of them moths?"

"Let me say it again," Mrs. Hallett replied. "I simply don't think that moths could evolve that way, which is why they would be found at the *entrance* of the cavern. But if you'll all follow me, I can show you a *real* troglobite. And I'd ask that we have no more questions about them until we reach that part of the tour. Thank you, girl in the red sweater."

Prickles of embarrassment tingled on Kristi's face. Even though she hadn't done anything wrong, she slowed down so that she was near the back of the group . . . walking next to Bobby. He gave her a knowing smile. "Hiding out back here?"

"Yeah, I guess Mrs. Hallett hates me now too," Kristi said with a short laugh.

"Then you're in great company," Bobby joked. "Seriously, you have to wonder why she gives tours to big groups of kids when she doesn't like kids, know what I mean?"

Kristi smiled. Maybe some part of her had known that Bobby would make her feel better.

Olivia hung back so that she could join them too.

"Why are you way back here?" she asked as she grabbed Kristi's wrist. "Come on—I don't want to face a troglo-whatever all by myself."

The kids pushed through a narrow tunnel to a wide

chamber that was brighter than the bats' cave. To her surprise, Kristi soon realized that they were standing around a massive underground lake. Its smooth, glassy waters reflected the lights on the cave walls.

"This is Crystal Lake," Mrs. Hallett announced. "It's the largest underground lake in North America, so large, in fact, that we're not even sure *how* big it really is. We have sent divers underwater and they have confirmed that there is yet *another* series of chambers within the lake, each one entirely flooded with water. It is impossible to even estimate how far down these underwater chambers go."

There was a sudden splash far across the lake; Kristi grabbed on to Olivia's arm as several of her classmates gasped. Mrs. Hallett laughed at their surprise.

"Now, now, nothing to be afraid of," she said. "The Crystal Lake is home to several varieties of freshwater fish, including a large school of rainbow trout. Of course, fishing is prohibited here. We also know that the darker areas of the lake, where there is no light, are home to several troglobites. You have heard me use that word often today. Does anyone know what it means?"

"Feel free to tell us whenever you're ready," Bobby

whispered sarcastically to Kristi. She grinned at him and tried not to laugh.

"A *troglobite* is an animal that has *adapted* over thousands of years to live in a light-free place," Mrs. Hallett said loudly and slowly. "Because they spend their entire lives in the dark, most troglobites are blind. In fact, many don't even have eyes. They're also usually white or translucent in color, having lost the pigment in their skin. You see, they don't need it to protect them from the sun's rays, since they're never exposed to a light source. In fact, if you tried to take a troglobite out of the caverns . . . it would *die*."

Mrs. Hallett paused dramatically. "We have a room over here where part of the lake is partitioned off so that you can see an actual troglobite for yourself! The room is very small, so you must come in groups of two or three, and very dark, so I'll use my flashlight to show you the troglobite."

Standing at the back of the group, Kristi assumed that she would be among the last to see the troglobite. But Mrs. Hallett pushed her way through the crowd and walked over to a small opening in the cave wall just a few feet from Kristi. It was hardly more than a crevice.

Mrs. Hallett's eyes focused on Kristi. "Red Sweater, since you're so interested in troglobites, would you like to go first?" she asked.

"Um, sure, I guess," Kristi replied as she glanced at Olivia.

The two girls squeezed after Mrs. Hallett into the tiny rock chamber. It was so dark that Kristi couldn't see anything, but she felt her legs brush against a metal chain near the edge.

"That's far enough," Mrs. Hallett said, somewhere in the darkness.

Then she switched on an industrial flashlight and pointed it at a shallow pool near their feet.

Kristi and Olivia leaned forward at the same time to take a closer look. It was just a fish swimming in tight circles around a too-small basin of water, but there was something so *wrong* about it—

With skin stretched tight over the sockets where its eyes should have been—

With translucent skin that seemed as fragile as a butterfly's wing—

And the narrow veins under the skin, where the pink blood streamed—

The chunk of muscle in its chest, its very heart, twitching, thumping, pumping—

The fish flinched as if the light pained it, and Kristi wasn't sure but she thought—she *thought*—it tried to swim away from the bright beam. And yet there was nowhere for it to go.

"Oh, don't hurt it!" Kristi cried out before she could stop herself.

Mrs. Hallett gave her a look. "It's just a fish," she said as she switched off her flashlight.

Kristi stumbled backward out of the narrow room, with Olivia right behind her.

"That was horrible," Olivia said.

"Seriously," Kristi agreed, nodding vigorously. "Why is this stupid field trip not over yet? I can't believe we were excited to come here. Now I can't wait to leave."

The girls crossed to the other side of the massive chamber, where more thin metal chains served as guardrails. Looking over the side, Kristi realized that this side of the chamber was bordered by a steep precipice.

"That must be one of those big drops Mrs. Hallett told us about," Olivia said. "I wish I had a rock or something. I would throw it down there to see if we could hear it fall."

"Ugh, at this point I don't even care how deep it is," Kristi said as she wrapped her arms around herself.

Olivia gave her a sympathetic look. "Don't worry, I'm sure it will be over soon," she said. "Remember, Ms. Pierce said our buses will leave no later than two o'clock. That's only a few hours from now."

"Hey," Bobby said as he and Tim joined them. "I don't know about you guys, but I don't think I'll ever eat fish sticks again."

Kristi smiled weakly at him. She tried to ignore the gleeful shrieks of surprise that echoed across the cave from kids who were seeing the trapped troglobite for the first time. It was taking a while for the entire seventh-grade class to see the fish; though Ms. Pierce and Mr. Tanaka tried to keep everyone quiet, the kids started talking louder and louder. Some of the boys were even messing around.

"Hoooo! Look at me!" shouted Nick Vincenzo. "I'm falling to my *doooooom!*"

Kristi spun around to see Nick standing right next to the thin metal chain that looped around the chasm.

"Nick, don't be stupid," she said. "Get away from the edge."

Nick gave her a sly look. "Ooooh, I guess I'm stupid. I guess I should be *so scared* of this *hundred-foot* drop," he said, mocking the worry in Kristi's voice. Then he stepped over the guardrail and balanced on one foot.

"Help! Help!" Nick cried in a whiny, high-pitched voice as he wobbled back and forth.

Everyone laughed, and Kristi knew that Nick was just goofing around. But the icy fist of fear grabbed her stomach and squeezed. She could see exactly how it would unfold: There would be a sudden *crack*, and a crumbling of rock beneath Nick's foot. Panic would career across his face. His hands would flail, grasping at the rusty chain as, in one fast and terrible motion, he fell. His feet—his legs—dangling into the pit, his waist hovering on the edge. The weight of his very own body would drag him toward certain death as gravity worked against him.

"Nick," Kristi said hoarsely. "Please."

He ignored her—or maybe he didn't even hear her. Either way, she seemed to be the only one who noticed the cloud of dust rising as ominously as smoke beneath his poorly balanced foot, or the clattering of pebbles as they plunged into the abyss.

And yet Kristi couldn't do a thing for him. As the fear rose into her heart, she could no longer speak; she couldn't even move. Just like all those years ago in the fun house, her feet were frozen. They would not do what she needed them to do. The horror of bearing witness to something so terrible, the *pointlessness* of it, the nightmare thought shrieking through her skull:

This is what it looks like when someone is going to die.

CHAPTER 6

A blur of red hair, a stocky body knocking into her, pushing her useless self out of the way, and everyone stared, open-mouthed, as Bobby hauled Nick back from the edge. Bobby clung to the other boy, breathing hard, his hands squeezing Nick's wrist. "You okay?" he said. "You okay? You okay? You okay?" He sounded like a parrot, or a broken toy, croaking out the only words he could seem to remember.

When Kristi looked at Bobby, she didn't see the ashen color of his face or the wetness on his cheeks or the sick twitch around his mouth when he swallowed. She only saw him for what he was in that moment: a hero. Bobby had saved Nick's life; she was sure of it.

Those pebbles *had* crumbled away beneath Nick's foot. Kristi knew that Bobby had risked himself for another while she had stood by, frozen and silent. Some faraway part of her brain thought with relief that, at last, Bobby would be treated with kindness. With respect.

At least, until Nick shoved Bobby away. He even kicked at him a little. "Get *off*," he spat. "You are such a freak. Are you *crying*? What is *wrong* with you?"

The echoes of the caverns made all the laughter seem louder than it really was.

Bobby furiously wiped at his face, but Kristi could still see the tear streaks. *Bobby was really scared*, she thought suddenly. *Really*, really *scared*.

Finally unfrozen, Kristi moved toward Bobby. She reached out a hand to help him up, but he shrugged away from her and pushed himself off the earthen floor of the cave.

"Bobby," she said in a low, urgent voice. "Forget Nick. That was brave. *You* were brave. It was amazing."

"Whatever," Bobby said with a loud sniff. He dragged his sleeve across his face, but he still wouldn't look at Kristi. "Nick is right—*I'm* the one who's stupid. He wasn't in any danger of falling."

"I think he was," Kristi argued. But Bobby had already started to walk away from her, staring at one of the tunnels like it was deeply fascinating. She was about to follow him when Olivia pulled her back.

"Kris, the tour is moving on," Olivia said. "I think we should get back to the group."

"Hey, there's some writing over here," Bobby said, sounding normal again. "It looks like . . . a sign, maybe? It's bolted to this giant rock."

"A sign?" Kristi repeated.

"Yeah," Bobby said as he stepped over the guardrail. "I'm going to see what it says."

"Whoa—wait a second. You're not supposed to cross the guardrail," Kristi said right away.

"I'm just going to read the sign," Bobby said. "I'll be right back. Promise."

Kristi, Olivia, and Tim waited in silence for a moment while Bobby squinted at the rusty sign. Its faded writing was hard to read. Suddenly Bobby called out, "It's a maze!" His voice was a little higher than usual. "This tunnel leads to a maze! Come on, let's check it out!"

"Seriously?" Olivia asked in disbelief. "No way,

Bobby. We shouldn't leave the group. It isn't safe. Mrs. Hallett said—"

"But look," Bobby interrupted her, pointing up. "There are lights all through here. She said that we can't go where there aren't any lights. The guardrails are just to keep us from falling into the pits and stuff. But there aren't any pits here. Just"—Bobby took a few steps forward—"just more tunnels."

Already his voice was sounding fainter and farther away. Something about the thinness of the sound, combined with the way her heart was still pounding, pushed Kristi to follow him. "Bobby, wait up," she said. "I'm coming with you."

He turned around to face her, about fifteen feet into the tunnel, with a look of delight on his face. "Really?" he asked, not even trying to conceal his surprise. "Awesome!"

"Yeah, me too," Tim suddenly said. "This tour is boring. A maze sounds a lot better."

"Hang on," Olivia spoke up. "What are you guys *doing*? Don't you think we should stay with the group?"

Tim shrugged. "Why would they turn on all those lights if nobody was allowed to go there? It's a maze.

Mazes are for kids, right? I'm sure it's safe. Maybe they just closed it for today since our whole class is here. But I bet it's fine for the four of us to explore it."

Just before she stepped over the guardrail, Kristi glanced behind her. She couldn't see the rest of her classmates; even the teachers and chaperones had moved on. Kristi turned to Olivia. "You coming?" she asked.

Olivia's eyes darted back and forth between the maze and the official tour route. Kristi had never seen her look so uncertain. "You said there are lights?" Olivia finally asked.

Kristi nodded. "Yeah. A bunch of them. As far as I can see," she replied.

"Okay," Olivia said. She stepped over the guardrail at the same time as Kristi, and the two girls walked quickly to catch up to Bobby and Tim.

Somehow none of them noticed the rusty old sign swinging from one post of the guardrail.

It read, simply, KEEP OUT.

"Do you think we're going to get in trouble?" Olivia asked nervously. "What if Ms. Pierce or Mr. Tanaka notices that we left the tour?"

"So what?" Tim said, flashing a smile at her. "We'll

just say we got separated and mixed up, and then we couldn't find the group. They probably won't even notice that we're gone. I bet this maze ends at the same place as the tour. That's how it usually works."

"What are you, some kind of maze expert?" Kristi joked.

"Yeah, practically," Tim said with a laugh. "I visit my aunt and uncle in the country every October, and they grow this sick maze out of cornstalks every year. Kids come from miles around to go through it. Now *that* is an awesome maze. I have a really good sense of direction. That's why I never get lost."

"Oh, then I guess we'd better stick with you if we ever find ourselves trapped in a cornfield," cracked Olivia.

Soon they had walked far enough that they could no longer hear the echoes of their classmates' voices.

"Are we sure this maze even goes anywhere?" Olivia asked doubtfully. "Maybe we're just walking . . . for no reason."

"You guys want to wait here a second?" Bobby asked. "I can go ahead and see. If it's just one long tunnel, we turn back now."

"If you don't mind . . . ," Kristi began.

"No way, it's cool," replied Bobby. Then he hurried down the tunnel, disappearing around the bend.

"I wonder how long he'll be gone," Olivia said, just to fill the silence. When no one replied, she grew quiet too.

A few minutes later Bobby returned, practically jumping around with excitement. "This maze is going to be really cool," he said. "Just up ahead, it splits up into four different tunnels. We can each take a different one!"

Tim immediately started messing with his cell phone. "Let's make it a race. I'll set the timer on my phone so we can clock everybody's times."

"No way," Kristi spoke up. "The last thing I'm gonna do is race through this cave. I know it's a maze and all, but it could still be dangerous."

"Yeah. I'm not sure we should split up," Olivia added. "Let's just stick together and pick one tunnel to explore."

"Here's the problem, though," Tim said importantly. "What if three of the tunnels are dead ends? It could take us, like, a *long* time to find the right one. But if three of us end up back here because our tunnels didn't lead anywhere, we'll know that the fourth person's tunnel is the way out."

"That's actually a good point," Kristi said. "Okay, I'm in. But I'm still not gonna race."

"Fine." Tim sighed. "I'll just time myself then."

"So, we're going to take separate tunnels, right?" Bobby asked, looking at each one of the kids.

Tim nodded.

Kristi nodded.

Finally, Olivia nodded too.

The kids didn't talk much as they followed Bobby to the four tunnels.

"Here they are," he said. "See you on the other side."

And then, one by one, they slipped into separate tunnels, disappearing down the narrow, twisting paths.

CHAPTER 7

Stupid, stupid, stupid, Olivia thought to herself as she walked through the lighted tunnel, kicking at the pebbles in her path. *We never should have left the rest of the class. We never should have gone into this stupid maze. And we never should have split up. Why did I agree to this?*

She had been walking for fifteen minutes now— or was it twenty?—on a downward slope through this unchanging rocky channel, and now she was at the point where she had to decide whether she should keep going . . . or turn back. And Olivia didn't have a clue which decision was the right one. If she was really just a few feet from the end of the maze, it would be so pointless to turn back now. And yet, if she was already lost—if continuing to walk would make her even more lost—

How long have I been in here? she wondered.

If she did turn back, Olivia reasoned, it would be another fifteen minutes (twenty?) back through this tunnel, then another ten minutes back to Crystal Lake, and then—what would she do? Retrace her steps back to the entrance of the cave and hope she could meet up with the group again? Olivia shuddered to think of walking back through the bat chamber all by herself, but she had no interest in going deeper into the caves, either.

So stupid, she thought again. *What were we thinking? Mr. Tanaka is going to be so mad at us. But what if the others already got back to the group? What if I'm the only one still stuck in the tunnel?*

What if they leave without me?

Olivia shook her head hard. *That's not going to happen,* she told herself. *They have a checklist of everybody who came on the trip. And Kristi wouldn't let them leave without me. She would never let them do that. No, I'll probably just get detention . . . for the rest of my life. And my parents will kill me.*

When the tunnel took a sharp turn to the right, Olivia kept walking. It seemed better to keep moving forward than to give up and turn back. She noticed that the tunnel was narrowing a bit and wondered if it would soon become a dead end. *I guess that would make the decision for me,* Olivia thought. Then, for the first time since she separated from the others, Olivia stopped.

What was that? she wondered. It sounded like . . . some sort of groaning noise—not quite human, but close. Olivia strained her ears, trying to hear it again, but all she could hear was:

Drip.

Drip.

Drip.

Olivia looked up and gasped in surprise. The ceiling above her was studded with the most astonishing crystal stalactites, glittering in the low light. Some of the stalactites were at least three or four feet long, narrowing into a razor-sharp point that could cause some serious damage to any unlucky person who stood beneath it at the exact moment it fell. Olivia suddenly remembered Mrs. Hallett's warnings about rock slides and the importance of being quiet. She vowed to walk even more carefully. The entire chamber was beautiful in a terrifying way, breathtaking and haunting, the sort of place that Olivia would have appreciated more in pictures than in person. Then she heard the groaning noise again, and . . .

Drip.

Drip.

Drip.

There it was again.

Olivia looked around with her eyes narrowed, wondering where the sound of water was coming from. Suddenly, her foot felt wet. She looked down and saw that she was standing in a puddle—and she had been standing in it long enough for the icy water to seep right through her sneaker. Olivia jumped to the side and shook her foot. *Gross,* she thought as she brushed against the cave wall—and felt more icy water soak into her sleeve. That's when she noticed the rivulets of water streaming down the cave walls. One or two rivulets—well, Olivia knew that would have been no big deal. But the amount of water flowing around her didn't seem normal, and for one horrible moment Olivia wondered if her tunnel had taken her directly under the Crystal Lake. She glanced suspiciously at the chamber ceiling. Was the rock above her thick enough to hold back millions of gallons of water? Or was it starting to crumble from millennia of erosion? Could the Crystal Lake be a little acidic—like the rainwater that had formed the Ravensburg Caverns? Would those lethal-looking stalactites come tumbling down in a rush of flooding water?

No way, Olivia told herself. *Remember what Mrs. Hallett said about the lights. They wouldn't have this section all lit up if it wasn't safe.* But she started to walk a little faster, just in case.

She felt something fall onto her head, a drop of water, probably, like the billions that had formed those stalactites over the years. Olivia shook her head, and then she felt another tiny tap, and then another. *What if this whole ceiling is about to cave in?* she worried, absentmindedly running her fingers through her hair to brush away the drops of water.

What she felt in her hair wasn't wetness though. There was something else perched up there. Something that was alive, and it wasn't *drip, drip* that Olivia felt on her head. It was *tap, tap.*

With a frantic hand Olivia slapped at her scalp and the living *thing* tumbled over her forehead, down the bridge of her nose, and landed at her feet, twitching. It was twitching because it was *alive*, though not entirely. She knelt down to look in fascinated horror at the thing that had been hanging out in her hair, tapping her head with its hairy legs.

It was a fat moth, thick in the body, with sharply pointed wings. Long antennae reverberated as the nasty *thing* tried to figure out where it was, and what had happened to it. Its frantic flailing made Olivia realize that the moth was blind, with empty hollows in the sockets where its eyeballs should have been. One of its wings was torn, but the moth didn't seem to realize that. Its useless wing flopped as the moth tried to turn itself over, but it was all in vain: Water was seeping into those fragile wings, dissolving them into a fine white dust that swirled on some strange current in the shallow puddle. A current, Olivia realized in disgust, that the moth was causing with its desperate, dying struggle.

She was rooted to the spot, looking at this miserable thing, with its bright-white wings and its body covered in thin, clear skin. Olivia didn't know how much blood would be in a moth's body—somehow the topic had never come up in her life science class—but it couldn't be more than a few drops. And yet it was enough blood for her to watch those drops flowing just under the moth's transparent skin, through an intricate network of tiny veins and capillaries, flowing slower . . . and slower . . . and slower . . . as the moth's life slipped away. Cold pinpricks of sweat broke out on her forehead and on the back of her neck. Olivia squeezed her eyes shut against the miserable, sick, swaying feeling she sometimes got right before she threw up. But Olivia would not throw up, she would get *out* of here, out of this horrible cave, away from this horrible *thing*. She had never meant to kill it, but there was nothing she could do now. Nothing but get away.

Olivia started moving faster, making more noise, completely forgetting Mrs. Hallett's warnings and her own worries. Again and again Olivia wiped her hand on her sweatshirt in case there was any powder from the moth's wings still on her skin. She felt a funny tickle on her hand. It was probably a loose thread trailing down from her sleeve, Olivia rationalized. Yes. That was it. A loose thread.

Except it wasn't.

Another horrible pale moth had landed on her skin, tapping . . . tapping . . . tapping with its hairy feet. She flung it off, and this time Olivia didn't stop to see if she had killed it or not. She didn't have time, because just a second later there was yet *another* moth—bigger than the others—nestled into a fold of her sweatshirt.

She slapped at the moth, but it wouldn't move, as if its feet were somehow stuck in the fabric. So when the next moth landed on her, that made two, and then there were three. Four. Five. A dozen. Moths too many to count, on her hands, on her shirt, on her jeans, on her neck, in her hair, in her ears—

Where are they all coming from?

What do they want with me?

For as long as she could remember, Olivia had hated moths. She was too young to fully recall sitting in her stroller at a summer picnic—but her mother had told her about that day so many years ago, when a large, hairy moth had landed on the side of her nose. It had stared at her with these glittery black eyes, and little baby Olivia couldn't get it off her face. She had started to cry. The memory came back to her now in hazy fragments; she almost didn't believe in it except it was so clear, so real, those bulging *eyes*—

That's when a new thought struck Olivia, one so horrible she almost screamed—but of course, she couldn't scream; she would end up with *moths* in her *mouth*. Already they were covering her eyes, making it hard to see; covering her nose, making it hard to breathe. But no matter what, Olivia would *not* open her mouth, which was why she couldn't scream when she realized that these moths, the ones bombarding her, didn't have eyes.

If none of them had eyes, then they couldn't see her. That meant they were finding her *some other way*.

Olivia was running now, but she couldn't outrun the moths. After all, they had wings. They could fly. They could follow her anywhere. They would never leave her alone. Even if she somehow managed to escape, Olivia already knew that the moths would be with her forever, in the memory of their crawly legs on her skin and their fluttery wings in her hair. The moths—were they really moths? Olivia wasn't sure anymore. What was it Bobby had said about radioactive mutants? Because surely regular moths couldn't get so big. Taller than Olivia. Taller than her father, even. So big that Olivia could see the grasping pincers in their mouths, the long hollow tongues flicking at her. And, Olivia soon realized in horror, the biggest ones hadn't completely lost their eyes yet. They were still blind, though; those hollow eyeballs filled with thick red blood that sloshed against the thin membrane. What did they *want* with her? Maybe these creatures were hungry. Maybe it had been a long time since fresh meat had stumbled into their chamber. Maybe that chain was strung up across the entrance to the maze for a reason, and Olivia had been too stupid to realize it.

Not here, Olivia vowed. *Not now. Not like this.*

Her arms windmilled wildly as she tried to cut a path through the horde of moths, not caring—not even noticing—all the little bits of moth bodies that got stuck under her fingernails: fragments of wings, whole antennae, hairy legs, and clumps of sticky powder.

She was almost there, almost across the chamber with its terrifying ceiling of treacherous stalactites, when Olivia realized that she had to make a choice. There were two parallel tunnels—one that looked bright and safe, with more lightbulbs burning than any other part of the cave she had seen so far. The other tunnel, though, was dark—so dark that Olivia couldn't tell if it was big or small, a true passageway or a just cramped room. For all she knew, the dark tunnel was nothing more than the precipice of a thousand-foot drop.

But Olivia knew one thing for sure: Moths love the light. If she looked closely at the bright tunnel, she thought—she was almost certain—that she could see the flickering shadows of fluttering wings. There could be hundreds, thousands, *millions* of moths congregating in that bright room. That made the decision so much easier. Maybe it wasn't a smart choice, but it was her choice to make.

And Olivia chose the dark.

CHAPTER 8

Tim didn't check the time on his cell phone. What was the point? It would only slow him down. Besides, it was so quiet in his tunnel. It wasn't like the corn maze, where the rustle of papery cornstalks was ever present, a quiet rattle underneath the shrieks and laughter of other kids. But deep within the Ravensburg Caverns, there was no way for Tim to know if his friends had already made it through the maze. The only thing Tim would gain from checking the time would be a little extra motivation to move faster—and he had plenty of motivation already. Tim wasn't sure why it was always so important to him to be first. It just was.

Besides, he had enough to focus on just getting

through the tunnel. The wide pathway for the guided tour had been worn smooth by thousands of feet traipsing over it for decades. This narrow corridor, however, was completely different. Jagged rocks jutted up from the floor; sometimes Tim had to jump or even climb over them, being careful not to scrape his hands on the rough walls of the tunnel. But Tim was sure-footed and swift as he sped through the maze; all those afternoons jumping hurdles and sprinting along the track were paying off. He felt good, confident. Of course he'd be the first one to get through the maze.

Then again, Tim had never expected to fall. How could he have guessed that one of those large, pointed rocks was precariously balanced on the ones below it? It looked like all the others, permanently embedded in the path. But when Tim tried to climb over it, the rock wobbled—then tipped—then toppled over, dumping him in a heap on the cold stone floor. It caused a small rock slide around him too—insignificant pebbles, sharp little stones, and a cloud of dust that got into his mouth and made him cough.

Only after the dust cleared did Tim realize that his ankle was throbbing. He must've twisted it, wrenched it in the socket as he stumbled off the cascading rocks. Tim winced ruefully as he rubbed his ankle, which was already starting to swell. *Not so smart, big guy,* he thought. *You'll be sitting out next week's track meet for sure.*

But Tim had bigger things to worry about now . . . like getting out of this maze on a busted-up foot. Well, so much for being the first one through the maze. At least it wouldn't matter if he came in last—not like in track.

Tim started rubbing his ankle more vigorously, hoping to increase the blood circulating through it. He thought he remembered Coach saying something about getting the blood flowing, back when Jason Morris messed up his foot during the first track meet of the season. Tim was about to get up and test his weight on his sore ankle when he thought he saw something move out of the corner of his eye.

More curious than afraid, Tim turned his head to get a better look. He thought those troglobites were pretty cool and, to be honest, he wouldn't mind seeing another one. Like some creepy blind lizard or something. But he soon realized that the thing that moved wasn't an animal. It wasn't even alive. It was just the last rock tumbling down from the pile.

But not a rock; at least, not like the others. Because this one glittered—glowed, almost—a deep crimson red. Red like fire. Red like blood. Tim didn't know much about precious gems, but he suspected it might be a ruby . . . a ruby the size of a quarter. Even Tim knew that it had to be worth a lot of money. His fingers clenched, imagining the cool weight of the ruby in his hand. It would be so easy to slip it into his pocket. It had obviously been buried for a long time. Maybe for *all* time. The ruby didn't do anyone any good stuck here underground. Surely no one would miss it, whereas Tim could get a lot for it. He could take it to that pawn shop a few blocks from school. And then—oh, the stuff he would buy! Those fancy new running shoes that claimed to boost your performance by 15 percent. A laptop for his big sister, so she wouldn't have to practically live at the library just to get her homework done. Something cool for his little brother, Jamie. And maybe he would shove a big stack of cash into an envelope and leave it in the mailbox for his mom. Maybe then she could quit her second job, the waitressing one that made her so tired all the time. When Tim saw her sprawled on the couch in her orange uniform that always smelled like salad dressing, asleep before she could even take her shoes off, it made him so *mad*. It didn't matter how many lawns he mowed or how many cars he washed; he could never earn enough money to really help her out. But maybe with a ruby that big, he could.

Tim remembered what Mrs. Hallett had said: Touch nothing, take nothing from the caves. And he knew, in his heart, that the ruby didn't belong to him. Maybe it didn't belong to *anyone*, but it definitely didn't belong to him. So after one last look of longing, Tim turned away and pushed himself up. He took a tentative step on his twisted ankle. It hurt, but not too bad. Tim limped a little as he walked a few yards. So far, so good.

Then Tim noticed another ruby, just a few inches in front of him. And a couple feet beyond it lay another one. He walked as fast as he could, somehow minding the pain in his ankle less when he realized that the floor was littered with rubies for as far as he could see.

He frowned as he tried to remember the history of the Ravensburg Caverns. Had any part of it been exca-vated as a mine? *Too bad Bobby's not here*, Tim thought. *I could ask him.* Mrs. Hallett had said something about early settlers searching for gold—but nothing that Tim could remember about rubies. *Then again, that makes sense,* he rationalized. *If there was a real ruby mine in here, they wouldn't want to tell people. Otherwise everybody who came in here would be trying to find a ruby to take home. Maybe that's why this path had been guarded off. They didn't want anyone accidentally coming across a fortune of rubies.* Tim remembered, suddenly, the lousy geodes in the gift shop—and the locked case of glittering red stones. His heart started pounding a little faster. That was it. That made perfect sense. There *had* to be a ruby mine deep within the caverns—and it looked like Tim had stumbled right into it. Literally.

There were so many rubies scattered on the ground around him, rubies in all shades of the sunrise—deep crimson and scarlet, rusty orange, fiery pomegranate. All sizes, too; some were as small as a pencil eraser. Others were as big as his fist.

Why *shouldn't* he take one?

Just one, Tim promised himself. *Not even one of the big ones. Just a medium-size one. For Mom.*

Tim knelt down and plucked one of the rubies off the floor. It was the size of a large gumball, it was perfectly round, and it was gorgeous. He smiled at the ruby and saw his own reflection smiling back at him.

Something strange happened then: His reflection in the ruby started to blur. It was almost like his smile was melting. Before Tim could look closer there was something suddenly wrong with his hand—a searing pain that was so intense that Tim couldn't cry out. It burned in the palm of his hand and in his gut, a pain so horrible that Tim couldn't even breathe. His instincts kicked in then and he dropped the ruby, just as flames burst from it.

The burning ruby rolled a few feet away and lay on the cave floor, spitting sparks and crackling angrily. Tim had to pry his fingers apart to look at his throbbing palm. There were black char marks still smoking in his tender flesh, but they were streaky and uneven. It almost looked like a laughing skull emblazoned in Tim's palm.

Tim blew on his burned palm, but it didn't do any good. He wished that he could plunge his hand into the Crystal Lake. It didn't matter what kind of troglobites swam through its murky waters; all Tim could think of was getting relief for his seared hand.

Flames were still leaping from the ruby—if that's

even what it was—and a single black plume of smoke curled up toward the cavern roof. Through the blistering pain in his palm and the throbbing ache of his ankle, Tim had a distant thought that he should probably try to stomp on the ruby. He shouldn't leave it smoldering in the caverns. But Tim knew that he could never find the courage to do that. He hated fire, *all* fire, even campfires and flickering candles on birthday cakes. It hadn't always been that way; Tim could still remember a time *before*, when he'd go camping with his dad and they'd roast hot dogs or marshmallows under the moon. But since that night—that brutal, heartbreaking night— Tim couldn't stand the stuff.

It was Christmas Eve. Tim was five years old. He tossed and turned in his bed, even long after Jamie was snoring peacefully on the top bunk. Tim wanted to stay awake all night—he was sure he could do it. He was determined to hear reindeer on the roof and Santa's footsteps in the living room. Of course he fell asleep though. He woke up suddenly, hours later, his heart already racing, wondering what presents were waiting under the tree. But something was wrong. Something was wrong in the air; it was heavy, too thick, too hard to breathe. The door creaked open and a big man crashed into the room. But there was no velvety red suit, no chiming silver bells. The big, shapeless man in his mask and his black jacket and his helmet swooped toward the bed, pulling Jamie out of the top bunk. Tim tried to scream, but smoke filled his throat and he choked, and by the time he could breathe again, Jamie was gone.

Then another big, shapeless man was in the room, hovering over Tim's bed, yanking him from the tangle of blankets and sheets. Tim was still holding on to Pup, the stuffed dog he'd slept with since he was a little baby. Tim clung to Pup as the man ran through the too-hot, too-bright house, where flames licked up the walls. It was happening so fast. The Christmas tree, the presents, the stockings—the worst bonfire Tim could ever imagine.

He never really understood how it happened—perhaps it was the shock or the fear or the jostling, uneven run—but just outside the living room, Pup fell from his arms.

"No!" Tim screamed. "No! No! No! No!" He had to go back for Pup. He tried to wrench himself free, but the big, shapeless man was too strong, and too determined to get Tim outside. Maybe he didn't hear Tim, or maybe he didn't understand him, or maybe he just didn't care. There was nothing that Tim could do but watch as the red-hot flames raced across the floor to Pup, devouring his brown-and-white fur, melting his brown marble eyes. Poor Pup.

Then Tim was outside under the cold, starry sky, outside with

Mom and Dad and Jess and Jamie, all of them wrapped in stiff blankets, a plastic oxygen mask strapped to Jamie's little face. So lucky, everyone kept murmuring to them. So lucky that they all made it out alive. They held tight to one another as they watched their whole house burn down. Everything was gone. Mom couldn't stop crying, and neither could Tim.

Since then, life had never been the same. And that's why Tim already knew that he would never be able to stomp out the burning ruby's flames. What he had to do was get out of the tunnel, get back to the group.

Then came a series of sharp *pops* that sounded like fireworks, and Tim thought, at first, that the rocky walls around him were cracking, about to crumble. It wasn't those rocks though. It was the rubies. They had all burst into flames: the big ones, the little ones, the in-between ones. All of them burning. And then, to Tim's horror, they started rolling, all on their own. All of them rolling toward *him*.

A wave of heat poured over Tim, rising from the floor in iridescent shimmers. Suddenly Tim understood exactly what was happening. Hadn't he always known? Hadn't he always, in some dark and unpleasant corner of his heart, expected this? The fire had come for him once before, and he had cheated it. Now it was back.

No, Tim thought wildly. *No, no, no, no, no.*

There was no big, shapeless man to save him this time. Tim would have to save himself. And he would— he *would* escape. It didn't matter how much pain he felt in his ankle; it didn't matter how hard it was to breathe; it didn't matter that the fear alone made it hard for Tim to remember what to do. That one driving impulse— *escape, escape, escape*—was enough to push him forward. He started to run. If there was one thing Tim did really, really well, it was run, even in circumstances like these. Sweat poured down his forehead, streaming into his eyes. He leaped over rocks as the fireballs pursued him. They seemed—Tim knew this didn't make a bit of sense—but they seemed to be aiming at him, as if they were trying to punish Tim for daring to run, for wanting to escape. Then the little fireballs rolled together into larger ones, feeding off one another's flames until a solid wall of fire pursued Tim.

Still he believed that he could make it. Still he believed in himself.

Until the tunnel started to narrow.

At first Tim thought it was his imagination, but all

too soon he realized that the tunnel was closing in on him: First it was five feet wide, then four feet wide, then three feet, then two. Then his shoulders were brushing against the sharp, rocky sides and Tim finally had to face the truth: If the tunnel continued to narrow like this, it would eventually become a dead end.

And the fire would win once and for all.

CHAPTER 9

As she walked Kristi was struck by how, well, *boring* the maze was: one long, twisty tunnel, the same unchanging beige rocks surrounding her for as far as her eyes could see. Which wasn't very far, to be honest. The electric lights were strung farther apart here, making them seem even weaker than the ones along the tour. The only sound Kristi could hear was the echo of her own footsteps; every so often she would stop and listen, straining her ears in an attempt to hear the others. To hear anyone, any*thing*. But the rock walls were thick and the silence was overwhelming. Kristi knew that she could scream and not a soul would hear her.

She started walking a little faster. She was ready to

be out of this maze and out of these caverns; she couldn't wait to be back on the school bus with Olivia. So far, the ride out to the Ravensburg Caverns had been the best part of the field trip. It would feel so good to be back in her own house; to sleep in her own bed.

Kristi started wondering if the others were out of their tunnels yet. She wished there was some way to know. She hoped that they would wait for her—she could imagine it now, finally emerging from her tunnel to see Bobby and Tim and Olivia standing around, looking bored. Olivia would grin at her and say, "Hey, you," like she always did, and Kristi would say—

"Hey!"

Kristi jumped. *Who said that?*

"Hey, you! In the red sweater!"

It definitely wasn't Olivia.

"Hey!"

The voice—whoever it belonged to—was coming from around the bend directly ahead.

"I see you over there!"

For a split second Kristi thought she should turn around and run—but to where? Besides, the person— whoever he was—had already seen her. He knew where she was. He could follow her if he wanted to.

"Please! I need help!"

There was something so desperate in the voice that Kristi found herself drawn to it. Her heart was pounding and her throat felt tight and swollen from fear, but Kristi knew that if someone was in trouble in the caves, she would help them. How could she do anything else?

"Wh—what's wrong?" she asked in a quavering voice.

"Come closer. I won't hurt you. I need your help."

Kristi pressed herself against the wall and crept toward the bend. She took a deep breath as she turned the corner and found another long, beige corridor made of stone. This one was not like the others though: Every five feet there was a square hole about three feet wide. And every hole was covered by thick iron bars.

"You came. Thank you," the person behind the first set of bars rasped. "I'm trapped and I can't get out."

"What happened?" asked Kristi.

"I was exploring the maze, just like you, but this door closed behind me and locked. I've screamed and screamed, but nobody has come to help. I don't think anyone knows I'm down here."

Kristi squinted at the iron bars, but it was so dark

and shadowy that she couldn't see the person behind them. "I'll go right now," she promised. "I'll run as fast as I can and tell them that you're trapped down here."

"No!" the voice shouted. "No, you can't leave! You don't understand what it's like to be trapped down here!"

Kristi swallowed hard. "But—I'm going to get help! I promise I'll be right back!"

"No!" he howled.

"What do you want me to *do*?"

A pale, trembling hand reached through the bars, pointing at the far wall of the tunnel. Kristi glanced behind her to see what the hand was pointing at. Under an exposed lightbulb hung a single key on a large ring. It looked very, very old, with flakes of orange rust peeling off its blade.

"The key is right over there," the man wheedled. "Right over there on the wall. Be a good girl and get it for me. I can't spend another minute in this cave!"

Kristi swallowed hard. Every molecule of her body warned her not to get the key.

"I'll go—I'll get help," Kristi repeated. Her mouth was very dry.

"Don't leave!" the man shouted. "Just throw me the

key! That's all you have to do!"

But Kristi couldn't do it. "I'll be right back," she said, and walked closer to the bars. "I give you my word."

Kristi looked inside the bars to make eye contact with the owner of the voice, to let him know that he could trust her, but just as she got close enough to smell the acrid old metal of the bars, he emerged from the shadows and pressed his face against the iron bars. "I just need the key," the man breathed. "Bring it to me."

But Kristi only drew in a sharp breath, horrified because in that terrible and unexpected moment she realized that it wasn't just a man trapped within the cell.

It was a clown.

And everything was so wrong about him, wrong in every way. The tattered ruffles around his thick neck. The dingy white pancake makeup pierced by unkempt stubble. The garish smears of red around his mouth. The cracked blue diamonds around his eyes. But the makeup wasn't even the worst of it. It was his eyes: tiny evil eyes, wild and unfocused and unfathomably dark.

"What are you doing?" he yelled. Kristi opened her mouth, but no sound came out. "Bring me the *key*!" the clown howled in outrage.

Kristi backed up in fear, further into the tunnel.

"Just bring him the key," another person hissed.

Who is that? Kristi wondered in horror.

"Why should that dirty old key just hang there?" the new person continued. "Just bring it to him. Or to me."

"Do it," a third person chimed in. "Do it *now*."

Kristi stared down the tunnel, wishing that she was wrong, wishing that it was all a dream. But it was real, too real, terribly real: every few feet a new cell had been carved into the thick rock, and every cell imprisoned a clown. They pushed their faces right against the bars. The smeary makeup made their faces grotesque, but what disturbed Kristi the most was their *eyes*, angry and evil. It must've been a trick of the light, the way the bulbs flickered off and on, because Kristi knew that there was no way for human eyes to glitter like that.

Kristi was all too familiar with what came next: A wave of icy terror that paralyzed her. She couldn't move a muscle.

What are they doing *here?* Kristi thought wildly. Then she remembered something that Bobby had said earlier—that circus—what did he call it? Circus Atrocitas? The fatal accident. The performers imprisoned in the caverns . . . and *never seen again.*

"Bring us the key," the clowns snarled. "Bring it!"

You. Are. Safe, Kristi thought, trying to overcome the fear that had seized her muscles. *They're all behind bars. They can't hurt you. They can't do anything to you.*

"Bring us the key!" all the clowns screamed at the same time. The first one started rattling the bars of his cell. "Bring it to us!"

Then, to Kristi's horror, the rusty bar crumbled to powder in the first clown's hand.

The clown stared at his hand in wonderment, as if he couldn't believe his luck. A chilling smile spread across his face. "Rattle the bars, boys!" he yelled. "Rattle the bars and free yourselves!"

Clang-clang-clang-clang-clang.

The sound was deafening, all those bars banging and the jubilant shouts whenever one disintegrated.

"Wait till I get out of here," one of the clowns shouted. "Just wait!"

"Maybe *she'd* like to be locked in one of them cells," another yelled. "We'll take the key and leave *you* here to rot, girl. How'd you like *that?*"

Kristi was still frozen as she watched those bars

come down, one by one by one. Soon, she knew, the first clown would be free. He would charge out of his cell, snatch the key, and free the others, too. And she would still be standing here, frozen in terror.

No I won't, Kristi vowed.

And she started to run. First she darted over to the key and grabbed it. This way if one of the clowns did get free, he couldn't just unlock all the other cells. They'd have to rattle themselves free, and that would take a bit longer, or at least Kristi hoped it would. Then she turned back and began to run down the tunnel.

In all her life, Kristi had never run so fast as she did past the jail cells of jeering clowns, through the narrow tunnel, away from those awful faces and rattling bars. Even when her muscles seized up with cramps; even when her chest burned and her lungs swelled and her heart felt like it was about to burst, Kristi kept running. Even when she started to stumble and had to pick herself up again and force herself to move forward, Kristi kept running.

And when she heard footsteps pounding behind her, Kristi ran even faster.

They were coming.

Coming for her.

More footsteps, running; more shouts and threats. Kristi tried to figure out how many clowns there were and how many had gotten free. But deep within her terror she still held on to the key and a ray of hope. She was young and strong and fast. She could escape from the clowns, escape from this maze, escape from this underground nightmare.

The tunnel twisted and turned sharply—once, then twice, then three times. Kristi had an uneasy sense that she was looping back around. If this part of the maze was an endless loop, she might really be running in circles—and if she was, Kristi knew it was only a matter of time before her body gave up. And she knew exactly what those awful clowns would do: lock her in a cell and throw away the key. Some of those bars weren't crumbling. Some of them were still strong. And once she was behind them, no one would know where she was. No one would come for her.

"No," Kristi said to herself. There *had* to be a way out, and she was determined to find it.

Especially as the footsteps behind her grew louder . . . and closer. They motivated Kristi even more, pushing her forward, even though she was starting to wonder how much longer she could keep up this frantic pace. Far ahead, off to the side of the tunnel, Kristi saw a dark crevice. It was narrow, but it might be just big enough to fit her if she squeezed in tight. *I can hide there,* Kristi thought. *I can hide there until the clowns stop looking for me. After they leave, I can go back the other way, past their cells, back to the Crystal Lake.*

Just having a plan made Kristi feel stronger. *I can do this,* she thought. *I can escape.*

In seconds, Kristi reached the crevice. She glanced over her shoulder but didn't see anyone coming. Kristi held her breath and squeezed into the crevice as the sharp rocks lining it scratched her face and hands. Then she exhaled heavily, shaking with exhaustion, fear, and relief.

I made it, Kristi thought. *I'm safe.*

Then, in the darkness, someone grabbed her hand.

CHAPTER 10

Kristi's scream was so loud and powerful that it threatened to rip her throat in two. A hand clapped over her mouth and she tried furiously to bite it, to twist away, to keep running.

"Kristi! Stop! It's me—it's Bobby—*ow!*"

It took a moment for Kristi to understand that she was hearing a familiar voice. A friendly voice. The fight drained out of her, leaving her muscles trembling and weak.

Kristi's legs crumpled beneath her; she sank to the floor and started to cry.

"What is it?" Bobby asked urgently. "What's wrong?"

"It was—it was *clowns*," Kristi sobbed. "So many of

them, and they're trying to get me. We have to *go*, we're not *safe* here—"

"Where?" Bobby asked. "In the tunnel?"

"Yes!"

"Stay here. I'll be right back," Bobby promised her.

"No! Don't leave me—"

But Bobby had already disappeared. One minute passed, then two. Kristi sat perfectly still, not daring to move, hardly even daring to breathe. What if Bobby *didn't* come back? The thought was so terrible that Kristi couldn't bear to think about it; she pushed it far from her mind. She crawled to the back of the crevice and felt the hole that Bobby must have come through. She pushed through it and stood up. For the first time since she had entered Ravensburg Caverns, Kristi found herself in an area with no lights. Not a single bulb dangled overhead. With a creeping chill, she realized what that meant: This area of the caverns was completely off-limits to visitors. And yet here she was, breaking all the rules like it was no big deal.

But the longer she sat there, the more her eyes adjusted to the lack of light. The room was almost entirely dark, but there were thin pinpricks of light that somehow pierced the rocky ceiling. Kristi couldn't see very far, but it looked like she was in a perfectly round room made entirely of stone. Some areas seemed even darker, causing Kristi to wonder if they led to more tunnels.

Then, just as he had promised, Bobby returned. He knelt down next to her and shook his head.

"They're gone, Kristi," he said. "Everything is okay."

Kristi knew that she should've felt better when Bobby said that. Instead, she burst into tears again.

"Whoa, what's wrong?" Bobby asked. "Don't cry."

"I-I'm sorry," Kristi said, trying to choke back her tears. "I was just—so—so scared—"

"Of . . . clowns?"

"Yeah."

Most people would've laughed—and in Kristi's experience, they usually did. But not Bobby. He simply asked, "How come?"

Kristi opened her mouth and closed it fast. It had been years since she had talked about what had happened in the fun house. Was she really ready to tell someone new?

Then again, she had a feeling that Bobby would understand.

"It happened a really long time ago," she began. "I was five years old, and my cousin took me to this carnival where her boyfriend worked after school. She made me go in the fun house by myself while she hung out with her boyfriend. She said it would be fun. But it wasn't. It was *horrible*. It was so dark, with all these spooky noises. And then . . ."

Kristi's voice trailed off, but she forced herself to keep going. "There was a clown in the fun house. His makeup and wig were really scary, not like a cheery birthday clown at all. And he . . . he started following me, from room to room. Everywhere I went, he was there, jumping out at me. I was trying to run away from him, but he thought he was hilarious. I was *terrified*. Eventually I ran into this room that was full of mirrors. Everywhere I looked, he was coming closer . . . and closer . . . but with all the mirrors, it was like a *hundred* clowns coming at me. I froze up. His hands were reaching out to grab me and I—I got so scared that I accidentally ran into one of the mirrors and broke it. It sliced up my arm pretty bad, and the clown got scared. He had to carry me out of the fun house, because I was totally lost, but I was so scared of him that I started screaming . . . and couldn't stop.

"When my cousin saw me all covered in blood, she *freaked out*. The manager of the carnival called an ambulance. And he fired that guy, too—the one who scared me so bad. The clown got really mad. He ripped off his wig and threw it on the ground. Then he leaned over and whispered, 'You're gonna be so sorry.'"

"Then what happened?" Bobby asked in a quiet voice.

"The ambulance took me to the hospital. I got seven stitches," Kristi replied. "But I couldn't forget about the clown. Every night, I hid under my bed and cried. One night, Mom came into my room to check on me and I got, like, hysterical. I finally told her everything and she helped me realize that I didn't have anything to be scared of. The clown at the fun house was just some stupid teenager. But I still hate clowns."

"*That's* why you freaked out about the grab bag," Bobby realized.

Kristi nodded. "Yeah. Stupid clowns," she said. "But you know, it's weird. . . ."

"What's weird?"

"Fear. Like, actually being afraid of something. It's hard to explain . . . but once you've been really, *really* scared, the fear can just *live* inside you. It's like it's always there, waiting to rise up and take you right back to the worst moment of your life. That probably sounds really stupid."

"I don't think so," Bobby replied. "It doesn't sound stupid at all."

Kristi tilted her head as she tried to get a better look at Bobby's face in the darkness of the cavern. He didn't sound anything like loud Bobby or goofy Bobby or totally-desperate-for-attention Bobby.

Then he started talking nonstop. "You know what I would've said if I'd seen those clowns? I would've been all, 'You're going DOWN, CLOWN!' And then I would've been all, 'Nice face, but doesn't your mom miss her makeup?' And then I would've been all, 'Nice car, but the preschool wants it back.'"

Kristi didn't think that Bobby's jokes were very funny, but she eventually cracked a smile. He grinned back at her and said, "Finally, my big mouth turns out to be useful."

"Sometimes I wonder about that," Kristi said carefully. "I mean . . . you can act totally normal, like everybody else. But then you can also get really loud and start showing off and stuff. How come?"

In the silence that followed, Kristi started to worry

that she'd hurt Bobby's feelings. "Listen, forget it," she said. "I don't even know what I'm talking about."

Bobby shrugged. "It's no big deal. I know people don't really like me," he said simply. "It's not exactly a secret that I don't have a lot of friends . . . or, uh, *any* friends. I guess I just figured that sooner or later, I'd make somebody laugh, and then somebody else, and then I'd be popular. That's why I did all that research before the field trip. I thought if I knew, like, everything about Ravensburg Caverns, people would be impressed. And then they'd want to be my friend. But maybe . . . maybe it doesn't work that way."

"Don't be silly. I'm your friend," Kristi replied. It was all she could think of to say, and it turned out to be just the right thing.

"Really? Cool," Bobby replied happily. He paused for a moment. "So, are you still afraid of clowns?"

"I'm actually not sure," Kristi said slowly. "I *thought* I was. But after being in that tunnel with all those clowns chasing me, I realized that I'm more afraid of freezing up. Like I did in that room full of mirrors. Ever since that night, I've been so worried that if something bad was about to happen to me, I wouldn't be able to escape. I wouldn't be able to save myself."

"But you did," Bobby replied. "You ran until you found a safe place. So now you know you can always save yourself, if you have to."

"Yeah," Kristi said, nodding her head. "I guess you're right." She paused for a moment. "So . . . what are you afraid of?"

Bobby paused for a long moment. Kristi could tell that he wasn't sure if he should tell her or not. At last, he opened his mouth. But before he could speak, he stiffened his shoulders. Kristi knew why immediately. After all, she heard it too: footsteps. Footsteps running in the dark. Running toward them.

"It's the clowns!" Kristi whispered in a panic. "They've found us!"

"No way," Bobby whispered back. "I walked through the tunnel for a while and I didn't see anybody. It was empty. Whoever you saw there . . . they were gone."

Kristi shook her head. "No, that isn't possible. There were so many of them. They were probably just hiding—"

"Hiding? Where?" Bobby asked.

"I—I don't know," Kristi replied. "Back in the cells, maybe."

Bobby looked confused. "What cells?"

Now it was Kristi's turn to look confused. "What do you mean, 'What cells?'" she said. "The clowns were in jail cells. There were, like, dozens of jail cells along the sides of the tunnel. All those clowns got mad at me when I wouldn't let them out."

"I didn't see any jail cells," Bobby said slowly. "The walls of the tunnel were totally smooth."

"But I *know* I saw them," Kristi replied. "I *know* they were there! I—"

"Okay, maybe I just missed them," Bobby said as he pulled himself up. "I'm going to take another look in the tunnel."

"Wait! Don't go. Not again," Kristi said.

"I should at least see who's coming," Bobby said as the footsteps grew louder. He glanced nervously toward the narrow entrance of Kristi's tunnel. "Don't worry. I'll be right back."

In an instant, he was gone.

Kristi crouched against the wall, ready to spring and run at a moment's notice. She could no longer see or hear Bobby, and it was worse—so much worse—to sit here alone in the dark. *He'll come back,* she told herself, partly because she believed it and partly because she wanted to convince herself that he would. *Bobby promised. And he wouldn't break a promise.*

But the footsteps were growing louder. And there was still no sign of Bobby.

Then an unseen force—heavy, hard, screaming—catapulted into Kristi. She slammed into the stone floor under its weight. She tried to push herself up, to escape, but whatever it was had her pinned. Her arms, her legs, her lungs all started to seize up with fear. Then Kristi remembered what Bobby had said:

Now you know you can always save yourself.

"Get *off* me!" she screamed as the blood started whooshing through her limbs again. Kristi was flailing and thrashing with all her might. *"Get off!"*

"Kristi?"

CHAPTER 11

"Olivia!" Kristi gasped.

Olivia rolled off to the side as Kristi sat up. She reached out for her friend and grabbed Olivia's arm as if to make sure she was real. "I'm so glad it's you," Kristi replied. "Are you okay? I didn't mean to flip out like that. I didn't know it was you."

"No, it's okay. I'm fine," Olivia replied, rubbing her knee. "I must've tripped right over you."

"Yeah, well, I was just sitting here, in the middle of the ground," Kristi replied. "So, your tunnel . . . it led you here too?"

In the dim light, Kristi could see Olivia nod. "Where *are* we?" she asked.

"I'm not sure," Kristi admitted. "Bobby was here, but . . ."

"But what?" Olivia asked. "Where did he go?"

"We heard footsteps, so he went to go check it out," Kristi explained. "That was . . . kind of a while ago."

"That was really brave of him," said Olivia. She shivered. "I don't know how he did it. I just know I'm not ever going into that maze again."

"Me neither," Kristi said fervently. "It was the *worst*."

"Was your tunnel really scary too?" Olivia said.

"Yeah," Kristi replied. "It was full of—"

Then she heard it again. Footsteps. Olivia heard it too.

"Maybe it's just Bobby," Kristi whispered.

"Or Tim," added Olivia.

To the girls' relief, it turned out that they were both right. Just seconds apart, Tim and Bobby entered the chamber from separate tunnels.

"Looks like we all made it, huh?" Bobby said as he sat down next to Olivia and Kristi. "I see Tim did not exactly come in first place. So, what's your time, Tim? Break any records?"

Tim winced with pain as he knelt beside the group.

"Not quite. I'm just glad that I made it at all."

"Why?" Olivia said. "What happened?"

"Well, first I messed up my ankle," Tim replied. "I think it's sprained or something. And then . . . You guys are gonna think I'm crazy. . . ."

"No, we won't," Kristi said, remembering the clowns and their cells. She was dying to ask Bobby what he had found when he ventured back into her part of the maze.

"There were these red rocks everywhere," Tim continued, making a split-second decision to leave out part of the real story. "They started exploding and bursting into flames. I thought I was gonna get burned to a crisp."

"Roast Tim," Bobby joked. "It's what's for dinner!"

Nobody laughed, and Bobby seemed to regret his words the instant he said them. "Sorry, Timbo," he said at once. "Not funny."

"I didn't know if I could get out," Tim said. "With my ankle and stuff. The fireballs were rolling after me, and the tunnel was filling up with smoke. It was hard to breathe, hard to see. But I noticed this crack in the cave wall and squeezed through it. And here I am."

"Fireballs?" Bobby asked doubtfully. "Are you sure?"

"Yeah, I'm sure," Tim replied. "Why?"

Bobby shrugged. "I don't know," he said. "But if there were a ton of blazing fireballs right over there, don't you think we'd be able to feel the heat? Or at least smell the smoke?"

Kristi didn't say anything, but she thought that Bobby made a good point.

"Well, how do you explain *this*?" Tim asked as he thrust his hand toward Bobby.

"Explain what?" Bobby asked.

"This burn on my palm," Tim told him. "I got it from one of the—oh!"

"What?" the others asked at the same time.

"It's . . . it's gone," Tim replied, staring at his hand in amazement.

An awkward silence fell over the group until Kristi turned to Olivia. "What was in your part of the maze?" she asked.

"Well, it wasn't fireballs," Olivia began. "It was . . . don't laugh . . . it was moths. Giant ones. They attacked me. . . . You know, 'moth' isn't quite the right word. Maybe they were trog—troglo—"

"Troglobites?" Tim helped her out.

"Yeah," Olivia said.

"But that's not possible," Bobby spoke up. "Mrs. Hallett didn't think that moths could become troglobites, remember?"

"I don't care what she said," Olivia said stubbornly. "She doesn't know everything. I mean, these . . . *creatures* were not normal. They were huge, and all white, and some were blind, but some had these freaky, bloody eyes. I honestly didn't think I'd make it out of that tunnel."

Kristi reached out for Olivia's hand and gave it a fast squeeze. "Mine was filled with clowns." And that was all she had to say for Olivia to understand.

"Well, I don't know," Bobby said. "Maybe it wasn't."

"What are you talking about?" Kristi asked. "Of course it was."

"I went back and looked all through the tunnel," Bobby explained. "There weren't any clowns. And no jail cells, either."

A flash of anger surged through Kristi. "So I guess I just made it up then," she said. "Like I made up the key I took off the wall."

"I didn't say that," Bobby said quietly. "But . . . where is that key, Kristi?"

"It's right—" she started to say. Then Kristi stopped.

Where *was* it? Hadn't it been in her hand this whole time? Surely she would've remembered if she had dropped it along the way.

But the key was gone.

"So what was in your tunnel, Big Man?" Tim asked sarcastically.

"Nothing," Bobby said simply. "It was just a tunnel. Like all the others we walked through."

"Well, isn't that nice for you," Tim said, rolling his eyes. "The rest of us were scared half to death—"

"Is that what scares you more than anything?" Bobby asked. "Fire?"

Tim looked away. "Yeah. Maybe."

"And you're afraid of moths, huh?" Bobby said to Olivia.

She nodded without speaking.

"So—and I'm totally not saying that you're making it up—maybe being alone in the maze was just really scary, and your imaginations ran away with you," Bobby said. "I mean, these caves *are* really freaky. And I was just talking all about Ravensburg Caverns' scary history—"

"Don't give yourself too much credit," Tim interrupted him. "I know what I saw."

"Me too," Olivia added.

"And so did I," Kristi said.

"It could even be that the air is bad down here," Bobby pointed out. "Like, not enough oxygen. That can cause hallucinations, I think?"

"And you're, what, immune?" Olivia said.

"I don't know—maybe the air was fine in my tunnel," Bobby said. "But I do know one thing: We have to get out of here."

"Well, I am *not* going back through that maze," Olivia said firmly. "No way."

"I think the best thing to do is retrace our steps back to the Crystal Lake," Bobby said. "There aren't any lights here. It might be a dead end . . . or worse."

"Forget it," Kristi replied, shaking her head. "I'm not going through any of those tunnels again either."

Bobby sighed with frustration. "We can all go through mine," he pointed out. "I promise there's nothing to be scared of. There was literally *nothing* there."

"You're sure about that?" asked Tim.

"Positive," Bobby replied.

"Okay," Kristi said decidedly. "Let's do it."

As she pulled herself up, Tim and Olivia did the

same. They followed Bobby back to his tunnel, keeping one hand on the cave wall to guide their steps.

"It's just through here," Bobby replied, glancing at them over his shoulder. "There's really nothing to worry ab—"

C-r-r-r-r-r-a-a-a-a-ck.

Then a deafening smash.

Before Kristi understood what the noises meant, she was coated in a layer of fine, powdery dust. She brushed it off her face, wondering numbly, *What is this?*

"Get back!" Bobby yelled, pushing Kristi and Tim and Olivia. "Get back!"

There was something in the air—smoke? No, it was clouds of dust that were illuminated by the thin light that streamed through the cracked ceiling. Suddenly the chamber was bright enough for Kristi to see the shower of pebbles that cascaded down from the ceiling, bright enough for her to see the massive rock that was now stuck in their way.

"Rockslide," Tim said, breathing heavily. "The ceiling caved in."

"I can't say for sure . . . but I think my tunnel is totally blocked," Bobby said. "We'll have to find another way out." He turned to Kristi. "I think we should try yours. I mean, I already went in it. There was nothing there."

"No," she pleaded.

"You'll be safe. You'll be with all of us," Olivia told her. "You can even keep your eyes closed the whole time—I'll guide you through it."

"Kristi," Tim said urgently. "We've really gotta get out of here. What if there's another rock slide? What if the whole ceiling collapses?"

"Okay! Okay!" Kristi said.

The four friends ran over to the crevice that led to Kristi's tunnel. She took a deep breath as she tried to psych herself up. *You can run,* Kristi promised herself. *You can run the whole way. You'll be out in a few minutes, and this whole nightmare will be over.*

But it didn't work out that way. This time, when the earsplitting *C-r-r-r-r-r-a-a-a-a-ck* came, Kristi and her friends knew exactly what it was. They jumped out of the way just as a wall of boulders fell from the ceiling.

Kristi leaned against the wall to steady herself. *Six more inches,* she thought sickly. *If I'd been standing six inches farther, I'd be buried alive right now.*

"The tunnels aren't an option," Olivia said. "We've got to find another way out!"

"We will," Bobby assured her. "I know we will."

It was light enough in the chamber now that Kristi could see across it to the other side. And in the very center, she noticed a dark, shadowy hole.

"What's that?" she asked, pointing with a trembling finger. "Wait, forget it, I don't want to know."

"We have to check it out," Tim said in a strained voice. "It's not like we have a choice."

They crept toward the edge. There were no guard-rails here, just a crumbling stone ledge that led to a pit of the deepest darkness that Kristi had ever seen before.

"How . . . how deep do you think it goes?" she asked.

"I have no idea," Tim replied. "I wish we had a flashlight."

"Does anyone have a coin?" Olivia asked suddenly. "We could drop it over the side to see if we can hear it hit the bottom."

No one answered her.

"You do, right, Tim?" Kristi spoke up. "From the diner this morning?"

"Oh, yeah. Right," Tim said. He fished a nickel out of

his pocket; it glinted in the silvery light streaming through the cracked ceiling. "So . . . do I just, like, drop it?"

"I think so," Kristi said. "Everybody, be really quiet so we can hear it land."

In seconds, they heard the *ping*. Kristi and Tim exchanged a glance.

"That actually didn't sound too far away," Tim said. "I think we could jump and try to find a way out from there."

"Are you crazy?" Bobby asked from the back of the group. "That sounded pretty far to me. This is a suicide mission. You can't just jump into a pitch-black hole. There's got to be another way out of here."

Kristi was about to argue when Olivia let out a shriek next to her.

"What is that?" Olivia cried.

Kristi leaned over the ledge and saw a pair of red, glowing orbs staring back at her. They flashed, blinked, disappeared, and reappeared—and then another pair appeared, and another—

Whatever had been sleeping in the pit was now awake.

"It's the clowns," Kristi whispered hoarsely. "Their eyes glowed like that."

"No, it's the moths!" Olivia argued.

"Are you both nuts?" Tim asked. "Look at the sparks! Those are fireballs!"

"What sparks?" Kristi snapped.

They might have kept arguing about it, but Kristi suddenly realized something. "Guys! I think—I think Bobby was right," she exclaimed. "This maze is every-thing we fear. None of it is real. How could it be? All of it somehow perfectly tailored to our deepest, most secret fears?"

When no one spoke, Kristi pressed on. "We have to jump," she said. "We have to face the—the scariest thing and *jump*. It really is the only way out."

"I don't know—" Bobby began. "What if—"

There was an ominous rumble in the rocks overhead.

"We have to get out of here!" Olivia shrieked, her voice high and almost hysterical.

"I can't!" Bobby exclaimed. "I'm not jumping into some dark pit! We can't even see what's down there!"

"But we *can* see what's up here," Tim told him. "A bunch of massive rocks that are about to collapse on top of us."

"He's right, Bobby," Kristi said. "We can't stay. We'll be buried alive."

"I can't jump!" Bobby replied, shaking his head wildly as he backed away from the pit. "I can't do it!"

"You can, Bobby, I know you can," Kristi said. "Here—hold my hand. We'll all hold hands and jump together, all of us at the same time. And whatever—whatever happens, we won't be alone."

She reached for Olivia's hand, then Bobby's. His hand in hers was clammy and damp, but Kristi didn't even care. Kristi squeezed Bobby and Olivia's hands. She wanted to reassure them. She wanted to reassure herself.

When Tim was holding Olivia's other hand, Kristi said, "Ready? One . . . two . . . three . . . Jump."

Kristi held her breath and stepped off the ledge, into the endless dark, where the blinking red eyes stared . . . and waited.

CHAPTER 12

In the instant she fell, Kristi felt something even worse than the swooping somersault in the pit of her stomach: Bobby's fingers, ripped from her grasp.

"Bobby!" Kristi screamed, reaching for him as she plunged through the darkness. "Bobby!"

Then: impact. She was on solid ground. It wasn't that far of a fall, after all. And there were no clowns, no moths, and no fireballs waiting for them at the bottom.

Olivia was sprawled on the cave floor next to her, crying softly. "We made it," she said, over and over again. "We made it."

"Bobby!" Kristi yelled again as she scrambled to her feet. "Bobby, *where are you?*"

Bobby's face, as pale and white as the moon, peeked over the ledge. "I'm—I'm here. I can hardly hear you, but I'm here," he called down to her. "Up here. I couldn't do it, Kristi. I couldn't jump."

"Don't worry, Bobby," Kristi called back, louder this time. "It's not so far. Just take a deep breath and do it."

"You don't understand," Bobby said. "I *can't*."

A groan of pain escaped from Tim as he touched his ankle.

Kristi knelt next to Tim and put her hand on his shoulder. "Are you hurt?" she asked.

His face was pulled tight from the pain, but Tim managed to nod a little. "I think—my ankle—it might be fully broken now," he said through clenched teeth. "But that's all. Everything else is fine. It's only my ankle."

"Okay, it's going to be okay," Kristi said, her mind racing. "We'll find a way to get you out." Then she turned to Olivia. "Liv, can you tell me what's around that bend? I have no idea where we are."

"You mean go *by myself*?" Olivia asked, shaking her head vehemently. "No. No *way*."

Kristi tried to control her temper. "Listen, Tim can't

even walk," she said. "Just go *look* around the bend."

"No, *you* go," Olivia shot back.

"Fine!" Kristi exploded. "I will! Bobby, just hang on, I'll be right back."

"Kristi?" he called, uncertain.

She ran as fast as she could toward the bend in the wall, where a faint light was streaming over the rocks. What she saw as she turned the corner seemed too good to be true. Kristi stood there, blinking in shock, with her hand pressed over her heart.

It was the entrance to the Ravensburg Caverns.

And just beyond that, the parking lot at the motel.

And even—Kristi could hardly believe it—two school buses, with their engines idling.

"Thank you," she whispered to no one in particular. "*Thank you.*"

Then she ran back to her friends.

"Guys! Guys! It's—you won't even believe—we're on the other side of the entrance. I could see our buses in the parking lot. We made it, guys, we really did!" Kristi cried, overjoyed. "Everything's going to be okay!"

"Are you positive?" Olivia asked as she scrambled up and threw her arms around Kristi, their fight immediately forgotten. "Are you sure?"

"Yes!" Kristi exclaimed. "We're, like, fifty feet from the buses! Tim, can you stand? Because I think—I think if you lean on Liv and me—"

"Yeah, absolutely," Tim said. "I'll crawl out of here if I have to."

Kristi was suddenly aware of a heavy silence.

"Bobby?" she called. "Are you still up there?"

"I'm here."

"Okay, listen to me," Kristi said, making her voice sound as calm and optimistic as she could. "All you have to do is jump. Then we'll leave this terrible place and never look back. That's all you have to do."

"But . . . is it far?"

"No! Not that far," Kristi said. "Look down—see us over here? It's seriously not far at all."

She waited for a moment, but Bobby didn't respond. Finally he said, "I can't see you. I can't see anything down there. It's completely black."

"Then . . . you'll just have to take my word for it. On my count, okay?" Kristi continued. "One . . . two . . . three!"

Nothing.

"Bobby?"

"I'm, um, I'm still up here."

"Dude," Tim spoke up. "Just, like, throw yourself over the edge. Seriously. Don't be a baby about it. You're making it so much worse than it needs to be."

"Shut *up*, Tim," Kristi muttered. Then, louder: "Bobby, let's try again. No counting this time. When I say 'jump,' go for it. Okay?"

"Okay. I'll try."

"Jump!"

Nothing.

Kristi took a deep breath and tried to stay calm. "Trust me, Bobby. You can do this. I *know* you can do this."

"I can't," Bobby moaned. "I can't do it."

It sounded like he was crying.

Suddenly everything made sense to Kristi: Bobby's panic over Nick's pretend fall; the way Bobby had stood as far back from the pit as he could; how hard he had tried to convince them to go back through the tunnels. She thought about Olivia wondering why Bobby was acting so obnoxious during the trip, and suddenly Kristi realized that Bobby wasn't excited about the caves. He was terrified of the drops in them. And he'd been trying to hide it all along.

"This is it, huh?" Kristi asked gently. "This is what you're afraid of. Heights."

"All my life," he replied.

"I know, Bobby," she said. "I know what you're feeling up there. We all do. But you have to believe me that the only way out is to face it—your fear—to look straight at it and take that leap anyway. And I promise you, Bobby—I swear to you—that you won't fall that far; that you'll end up down here with us, safe and sound, and we'll all go out to the buses together.

"And you know what else?" Kristi continued. "Your fear of heights—this is the worst it will ever be, Bobby. Because once you jump, once you feel that terror washing over your whole entire body and you do it anyway, you'll know"—Kristi's voice caught in her throat—"you'll know that you can do *anything*."

"I don't know how to do it," Bobby replied. "I don't know how to jump. I'm standing right here, at the edge, and I keep telling myself 'Jump, dummy! *Jump, idiot!*' and I can't. It's like my feet are glued to the ground."

"You're not an idiot. You're just scared," Kristi said urgently. "But listen, Bobby. Do you trust me?"

"Yeah. Definitely."

"Then make this jump. Do it for you, do it for me, do it for all of us. The buses are outside. They're ready to go. Don't you want to go home? I really want to go home, Bobby. Please. Just jump."

"Okay, Kristi," Bobby said, and he suddenly sounded stronger and more certain. "Okay. I can do this. I'm gonna do this."

"Yes!" she exclaimed. "You can!"

"Right now," Bobby said. "One. Two. Three."

Nothing.

Suddenly Kristi turned to Olivia. "Did you hear that?" she asked in a strangled whisper.

"Bobby?" asked Olivia.

Kristi shook her head. "No. Listen."

At first both girls heard only Bobby's quiet sniffles. Then, as if carried on a far-off wind, came a low wail that was soon joined by several other voices. Children's voices.

Kristi looked at Olivia with wide eyes. "That's it," she said. "That's the sound we heard last night."

"Oh, Kris. I think . . . I think you were right," Olivia said. "It *is* the kids. The lost ones . . . the ones who disappeared so long ago."

The ones who were never found, Kristi thought, but she couldn't bear to say it. *The ones who were too afraid to face their fears.*

Kristi stared up at the ledge, but she couldn't see Bobby's face anymore. "Bobby," she ordered. "Jump. Right now. Do it."

"I feel funny." Bobby's voice sounded hollow and far away. "I don't feel—something's not—I can't—I can't see my hands—"

"You can't see *what?*" Kristi yelled.

There was no answer.

"Bobby!" Kristi cried. "Are you there?"

"Don't . . . leave. Don't . . . leave me here." His voice floated down to her. "Don't . . ."

The moaning grew into a cacophony of howls that made Kristi want to cover her ears and cry. "*Bobby!*" she yelled. "Please jump! You have to jump right now or I don't know what will happen to you! Please, Bobby, *jump!*

"Bobby? Are you still there?

"*Bobby?*"

Beads of sweat dotted Kristi's forehead; she gritted her teeth with determination. "I'm not going to leave you, Bobby," she promised. But even as she spoke the words, doubt swelled in her heart. How could she possibly find him?

"Bobby!" Kristi screamed. "I'm coming! Just hang on!"

Still there was no answer.

Would there ever be again?

DO NOT FEAR—
WE HAVE ANOTHER CREEPY TALE FOR YOU!

TURN THE PAGE FOR A SNEAK PEEK AT

You're invited to a

CREEPOVER®

The Ride of Your Life

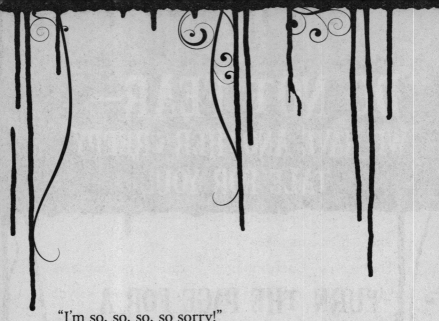

"I'm so, so, so, so sorry!"

Gabby Carter had just jumped out of her seat to hand her meal tray to the flight attendant, and she figured she would hand in her neighbor's tray as well. But leaning over made her tray table bounce into the air. Which had caused her drink to bounce into the air as well. Cranberry juice rained down the tray, dripping onto the floor and Gabby's armrest and the cover of the magazine that the woman in the seat next to her had been reading before she fell asleep.

"Sheesh. I just wanted to help without waking you up," Gabby said miserably.

"Well, you didn't," snapped the woman, who was all

tucked in for the flight. She had taken off her shoes and replaced them with woolen booties. She also had a sleep mask pushed up onto her head and a neck pillow resting on her collar. In other words, she didn't seem to care how crazy she looked. "I'm perfectly capable of turning in my meal tray by myself. And anyway, I wasn't sleeping."

"You were *too* sleeping!" Gabby protested. "I heard you sno—breathing deeply."

The woman glared at her. "I was resting my eyes. And I *needed* the rest, sitting next to you. Look at you. We practically just took off, and your seat already looks like a bird's nest. I can't believe they gave me a seat next to a child."

"We'll have everything back to normal in no time," said the flight attendant. He was a youngish man, and he looked as if nothing ever bothered him.

"Let's just clean up a little here," he said, "and we'll all be as good as new." From somewhere in his cart, he pulled out a damp towel and deftly began to mop up the spill. He glanced at Gabby. "Why don't you sit down and fasten your seat belt again?"

Gabby sat down. *An hour into the flight,* she thought, *and already I'm causing trouble.*

"And you, ma'am—would you like something else to read?" the flight attendant asked the woman next to Gabby.

"No!" she snapped. "Just take this away." She handed him the juice-stained magazine. Then she pulled a book of Sudoku and a pencil out of her purse and bent over the page with angry concentration.

"Is this your first flight?" the attendant asked Gabby.

Gabby sighed. "No. My sixth. And I've spilled something on every trip."

"Sometimes it's hard to sit still," the flight attendant said. "Anyway, I'm Toby." He gestured down at his name badge. "As I guess you already know."

"I'm Gabrielle," said Gabby. "Gabby for short."

"And where are you headed, Gabby? Besides Iowa, I mean."

"I'm going to visit my best friend, Sydney," Gabby told him more cheerfully. "She lives in a town called Trouble Slope. Have you heard of it?"

"I don't think so. Is it close to Des Moines?"

"It's, like, a two-hour drive," said Gabby. "My aunt lives in Des Moines, so she's going to pick me up at the airport and drive me to Trouble Slope. It's a pretty small town. But it does have a college," she added. "That's where Sydney's parents work. They're both professors, and Trouble Slope was the only college they found that could hire both of them at the same time."

She sighed. "So that's why they moved out of San Francisco a year ago."

To Gabby, it had felt like the longest year of her life. She had other friends, of course, but she and Sydney had been *best* friends since kindergarten. It hadn't been hard to stay in touch since Sydney had moved. The girls had texted or video-chatted pretty much every day. But texting and video-chatting were just not the same as having Sydney actually live in San Francisco.

"What's Sydney like?" Toby asked sympathetically.

"Sydney is—Sydney is *calm*," Gabby told him. "That's one of the best things about her. She never seems to worry or get flustered. She never leaves anything till the last minute. She's never late. She's the total opposite of me."

"Sounds as if you make a good team," Toby said. "She's calm, and you're—uh—energetic."

"Exactly! Sydney usually *likes* it when I do something crazy. Because she never would have thought of it."

"Well, I hope you have a—"

A voice suddenly broke in—the voice of the cranky woman next to Gabby, of course. "Don't you have anything to do besides stand here?" she asked Toby.

For a second, Toby looked startled. Then he arranged his face into a smile. "I'm sure I do," he said. "Thanks for the reminder. Can I get either of you anything before I go back to work?"

"You already asked me that," said Gabby's seatmate.

She is really *rude,* thought Gabby. It seemed as if the best thing she herself could do was not to give Toby any more trouble. "I'm fine," she told him. "But thanks for listening."

"My pleasure," said Toby. Then he leaned over and pointed at the cranky woman's Sudoku.

"That should be a five, not a three," he said. He winked at Gabby.

As Toby headed up the aisle, Gabby silently vowed that she would sit without moving for the rest of the flight. She wouldn't even use her half of the armrest. She would give her seatmate absolutely nothing to complain about. . . .

Gabby had been up late packing the night before.

Sitting motionless now, she felt her eyes starting to close. She had just one more thought before falling asleep.

I hope I don't end up leaning on that lady's shoulder.

"We're landing. Wake up!"

Once again the woman next to Gabby was making her presence known.

Gabby straightened up, rubbing her eyes. "We're landing?" she echoed in a blurry voice. "I slept for three hours?"

"Yes. You missed the movie. And the snack."

The woman's eyes rested on Gabby for a second. "I've been to Trouble Slope several times," she added abruptly. "I'm very well acquainted with that place."

Still groggy, Gabby struggled to sound polite. "You— you have? I mean, you are?"

"I had family there," said the woman. "They moved out as soon as they could."

"Is it a nice place?" Gabby felt stupid the minute the question was out.

"It certainly is not. It's dangerous."

"*Dangerous?*" Gabby echoed. She was wide awake now.

"That's what I said," the woman replied curtly. "It's especially dangerous for children. You'd be better off if you turned around and went home right now."

Before Gabby could answer, the plane touched down on the tarmac and came to a stop. Everyone started bustling around—including the woman next to Gabby, who jumped to her feet and pushed into the aisle ahead of all the other passengers.

Which was just as well, since Gabby hadn't come up with a response to her strange warning.

What a weirdo, Gabby thought as she reached down for her backpack.

Because come on—how could a tiny town in the middle of nowhere possibly be dangerous?

Aunt Lisa spotted Gabby the minute she stepped into the baggage claim area. "Just look at you!" she marveled after giving her niece a hug. "I swear you've grown three feet since I saw you last. Are you hungry, by any chance? I know we're two hours ahead of California time, but—"

"I'm *starving,*" Gabby interrupted. "I feel like I ate lunch three days ago." She pulled out her phone to check the time. Seven o'clock. The plane had been right on schedule. And even though it was only five o'clock back at home, she was dying for supper.

"Let's eat here at the airport, then," said Aunt Lisa. "There won't be much besides fast food once we're out of Des Moines."

"It was really nice of you to pick me up, Aunt Lisa," Gabby remembered to say a few minutes later as she and her aunt studied their menus. They had found an airport restaurant, the Palm Palace, which was doing its best to persuade its customers that they were in sunny California. The tables were made out of surfboards, and a few pairs of flip-flops had been scattered around for realism.

"I was happy to pick you up!" replied her aunt. "I just wish I could see you for a real visit. If I didn't have this stupid work trip the day after tomorrow, I'd keep you for a couple of days. I'm glad it's a two-hour drive to Trouble Slope so we can catch up."

"Aunt Lisa, have you ever heard anything . . . bad about Trouble Slope?" Gabby asked.

"Bad? What do you mean?"

"Well, this weird lady was sitting next to me on the plane, and she said it was dangerous there."

"Dangerous?" Aunt Lisa echoed. "A university town miles from any city? I'm guessing it's one of the safest places in the United States. What did this woman say, exactly?"

"Oh, she said a lot of stuff." Quickly Gabby ran through the story of her unfortunate encounter. "Spilling that juice was the most embarrassing moment of my whole life," she said.

Aunt Lisa gave a little cluck of irritation, but not because of Gabby. "That woman sounds awful. I'm sorry you had to spend the whole trip next to her."

Gabby giggled. "She was probably sorry she had to spend the whole trip next to me! Anyway, I'll stop thinking about it. Sydney would tell me there's no use worrying about stuff that's in the past. And I want to get into Sydney-mode before I see her. Oh, I can't wait!"

"Let's order dessert right away, then," Aunt Lisa suggested.

Gabby thought that would be a good idea.

"And now to remember where I parked my car," said Aunt Lisa when they had finished their ice cream (raspberry sorbet for Aunt Lisa, brownie batter for Gabby). "It's not always easy to spot—it's not that big."

That was an overstatement. Or was it an under-statement? Aunt Lisa turned out to have the tiniest car Gabby had ever seen—a green two-seater that looked about three inches tall. There was barely room for the two of them plus Gabby's backpack and suitcase, but after a short struggle, they managed to squeeze every-thing in. Aunt Lisa dug around in her purse until she found her parking receipt.

"Why bother waiting in line?" Gabby asked as they approached the ticket booth. "You could just drive under the cars ahead of us."

It was true that Aunt Lisa had to reach way, way up to hand the money to the parking-lot attendant.

"I hope you don't have a long way to go in that lunch box," he said as he passed back some change and a receipt.

"Just a couple of hours," said Aunt Lisa. "We're going to a place called Trouble Slope."

She edged the car forward, waiting for the mechani-cal arm to lift. "And . . . we're off!" she said to Gabby. "In two hours, you and Sydney will be together again."

WANT MORE CREEPINESS?

Then you're in luck, because P. J. Night has some more scares for you and your friends!

In the story, Kristi and her friends have to confront their own personal worst nightmares. What's your worst nightmare? Draw a picture of it in the box below, if you dare!

YOU'RE INVITED TO . . .
CREATE YOUR OWN SCARY STORY!

Do you want to turn your sleepover into a creepover? Telling a spooky story is a great way to set the mood. P. J. Night has written a few sentences to get you started. Fill in the rest of the story and have fun scaring your friends.

You can also collaborate with your friends on this story by taking turns. Have everyone at your sleepover sit in a circle. Pick one person to start. She will add a sentence or two to the story, cover what she wrote with a piece of paper, leaving only the last word or phrase visible, and then pass the story to the next girl. Once everyone has taken a turn, read the scary story you created together aloud!

I never intended to get separated from the rest of the class when we went on a field trip to visit the historic _____ Mansion. But I did, and it was the scariest day of my life! I wandered through the house like I was trapped in a maze. Every room was creepier than the one before.

And the last thing I expected to see was what I
stumbled upon in the attic. There I saw...

_____

_____

_____

_____

_____

_____

_____

_____

_____

_____

_____

_____

_____

_____

_____

_____

_____

_____

THE END

A lifelong night owl, **P. J. NIGHT** often works furiously into the wee hours of the morning, writing down spooky tales and dreaming up new stories of the supernatural and otherworldly. Although P. J.'s whereabouts are unknown at this time, we suspect the author lives in a drafty, old mansion where the floorboards creak when no one is there and the flickering candlelight creates shadows that creep along the walls. We truly wish we could tell you more, but we've been sworn to keep P. J.'s identity a secret . . . and it's a secret we will take to our graves!